Thorsten Schelberg

AF281926

The shield of 10000 years

Translated by deepL(free version, but I am going to donate, promise) and the author's mediocre English abilities.
Mistakes are on me.

For Nina, Thalia and Jürgen.
Even if you are never going to read this fine piece of literature.

Prologue

"They're coming."
"Yes."
"Is there a chance?"
"Yes. One."

Part one
Awaria

'Meditation is a war.'
He stands threateningly in front of When.
An strongroom made flesh, and When wonders what combination of numbers he needs to put him into rest mode.
'Forget everything you've ever heard about meditation. Forget that ridiculous term.'
His eyes bore into those of the young student.
A bodybuilder, but in the robes of the Gelugpas, fresh from a retreat in the Himalayas.

Where they apparently ate children and paid homage to Kali,
When surmises, and can't suppress a smile.

'Did I say something funny, student?'

When feels his own power. Untamed at first. Then focussed, like a laser.

We can both play this game.

And the boy returns the gaze. Until needles pierce his limbs and he has to look down.

He gasps. He almost suspects that blood is leaking from his nose.

'Ahhh, the child prodigy. I see.'

Cremp turns to the blackboard, and the students wonder where he got it from.

'Forget everything. Meditation. Books on meditation. Sutras, religions, saints, would-be teachers who once patted you on the back approvingly.'

He turns back to the students, suddenly holding a Zen staff.

'And above all, forget who you are. Your names, origins, friends, parents.'

He takes a quick look at When.

'When you were first blessed, what exams you took, what you achieved, what you tried, what you failed at. What honours you have on your wall, what you do for the environment, what secrets you think you have to keep.'

His voice becomes a dull roar.

'Believe me, students. This has all been done before. All of it.'

The staff shoots out in a flash, striking a girl between the neck and shoulder blades.

When remembers her golden curls, her big eyes, into which tears are now shooting.

'But don't forget one thing. Your posture.'

His gaze is palpable on his skin. When's back tightens mechanically. He doesn't even dare look round, but his classmates are certainly tensing up too.

'Straight spine. Whether you're in the Himalayas or in the heart of Africa. Or in one of your beauty and spa water tanks ... straight spine. The rest is secondary.'

The wand snaps forward. When it hits Goldilocks again, When almost has to laugh.

If he had known back then how painful something like this would feel, and how often he would have this pleasure ...

He wouldn't have laughed.

End of lesson.

You can almost hear the room breathing a sigh of relief.

Then the headmaster enters. 'This is just the beginning. Too high expectations could destroy everything.'

The veteran looks at him sharply. 'Too low expectations might as well.' He looks out of the window into the rain. 'Time is running out. The more peaceful we become, the greedier and more brutal our neighbours get. It's not the first time I've experienced this.'

The headmaster nods in agreement. 'So, will they survive? The training?'

Cremp glances at the Zen staff. 'Physically, yes, if that's what you mean.' He puts it aside. 'If you mean the potential of them, I have my doubts. They're all hard-working. Persevering. Calm.' He glances at the empty chair by the window. 'Well, yes. Almost all of them.'

The headmaster follows his gaze. 'You're talking about her brother?'

'Yes. He's going to be a piece of work. And we have so little time. It's going to be hard.'

'But...?' The headmaster sees a flash in his counterpart's eyes.

'I've challenged him to a duel.'

'You what? The students are sixteen. And we picked him up

off the street, he's got far less experience than anyone.'

The veteran waves it off. 'Nothing happened to him. He dropped out before I could finish.'

'And?' asks the director curiously.

'And the millisecond before, he nearly knocked me out of my shoes.'

The Viktualienmarkt.

No storms today, which has rarely happened since the end of the 2020s.

Noise creeps through the streets, but doesn't reach him. Perhaps because of the statue. It is her, in her final, heroic pose, her hand raised imperiously.

When When was young and on the streets, this had always been the place with his favourite tourists. Who he and his friends loved to relieve, so that the journey home in beer bliss and hung with souvenirs would no longer be quite so arduous.

He looks down at himself. Wearing a uniform, like the policemen, who had tried in vain to follow him through the alleyways. Strange, he thinks to himself.

'Brother,' a gentle voice brings him back to the present.

I wonder what his masters at the academy would have said about these mental excursions.

'The tanks are ready.'

He nods and follows his brother up Old Peter. Which is really old, and with the best of views.

Meliannenplatz.

A crowd surges back and forth, waiting for their hero.

'How long now?'

When focuses his gaze, taking in details of individuals.

'Forty-seven minutes since the first significant groups arrived.'

'Were there any riots?'

'Yes, but few. You know how he plans it.'

He nods. The waiting, the pressure on the cauldron, before the big show.

'We used a Sister of the Hand unit to prevent anything worse. But had to pull it off.'

A mischievous smile flies across his brother's face, reminding him that they are only human too.

'Too many enemies?' asks When.

Hardly. The months he spent training with them were some of the most painful of his life. Aikido. Defensive fighting style. As if, he thinks.

'There are limits even to their abilities. Apparently at some point there were so many opponents that they ended up running into each other. Or into their own kicks. It did get a bit bloody.'

When nods in understanding as he continues to watch the crowd down there.

'He's coming.'

Applause erupts.

When is not in his sensitive mode, but even a stone could feel the rising tidal wave. The anger. The hope. It all rises with him.

The Tribune takes the stage almost humbly, only looking up when he stands at the lectern.

He has become a man of the people. He has swapped his suit for a 'Will to Resist' tracksuit, his brown leather shoes have given way to trainers. From country leader to rebel in just a few years.

He is certainly changeable, When thinks.

And when the Tribune raises his arms and gives the crowd a look, When feels his brother's breathing becoming irregular.

'Citizens.'

Everything falls silent.

His voice sounds melodic but firm. Bright, but with an underlying baritone.

Our brothers of the middle way should study you. At least some aspects of you, my friend.

'Citizens!' This time it sounds like an appeal, almost pleading. 'How I wish I could call you friends, even brothers or sisters. But these words, once so beautiful, so meaningful, have been destroyed.'

Slowly, he raises his hand and, like a cleaver, jerks his finger towards two brothers of the Order who are flanking the crowd at the edge of the square, looking strangely unconcerned. Perhaps because they are hopelessly outnumbered.

'By them.'

Shouts of protest, hands shoot into the air, and When can feel the hatred creeping up. Perhaps there are a few agitators among them, but certainly fewer than expected.

'Should we start? Before it gets worse?' His brother beside him has regained his composure.

'Not yet,' says When, without averting his gaze.

Let him let off some steam first. Find the culprits, whip up the mob. Shoot your powder first.

'Look around you, my dear citizens. Look right and left,' the Tribune demands.

The crowd follows his order uncertainly.

'What right, what freedom are you allowed to enjoy right now?'

Seconds pass. Questioning looks are exchanged. And When knows exactly what is coming.

'The right to stand, citizens!' he shouts. 'The right to stand!' he repeats and has the crowd again. 'And do you know who no longer has this right, my dear citizens?'

When takes a deep breath. Our children.

'Our children!' roars the speaker. 'And why? Because this government obliges our children, obliges them to waste hours of class time doing nothing. Nothing! Just sit. In some pose that a short-legged Indian once used thousands of years ago, sitting lazily under a tree.'

When senses a movement next to him. 'That's not true! You do...'

'Quiet, brother,' he interrupts him. His voice is a whisper.

'Forgive me. It's just ... I'm sorry.'

When smiles. 'I know. And the studies prove it. But the best proof that meditation works for children is you.' He gently takes his hand. Feels the calm return. 'Yes, brother.'

'What should we do?'

'Enjoy the show a bit more.'

His smile shouldn't be there. Deep meditation takes a long time to prepare for, his instructors have always said. No, When knows now. It needs humour.

'But that's just the tip of the iceberg!' continues the righteous avenger, now really in a rage. 'They have destroyed our traditions in all areas! Our ways, those of our beloved ancestors. And for what? Not for prosperity, my friends, that's for sure!'

He demonstratively pulls out the inside of his trouser pockets and laughs.

'They've taken travelling away from us. The opportunity to see other countries, other cultures. And they call that respect! They've taken away our cars, our pride as an economic nation - in the name of environmental protection!'

His voice gets louder and louder and storms inexorably towards the climax.

'And we're being controlled!'

Suddenly When has the feeling that the Tribune is looking directly in his direction.

'By the freaks this grotesque system has produced.'

The clamour of the crowd hurts his ears.

'It's time, brother. Prepare the tanks,' says When.

Freaks..... He smiles. Glides down. You haven't got a clue, my friend.

'Second step: Tranquillity.'

Later that year.

There are no casualties yet, at least not physically. But some have thrown in the towel and are now serving in other areas, as far away from the living safe as possible; somewhere soft and nice smelling. And well, quiet.

'What is that, anyway? Tranquillity?' Cremp shouts as he pushes the volume control on the sound system up again.

Anything but this, thinks When and looks at the tense faces of his sisters and brothers. Goldilocks is still there. So is his friend; and a Japanese guy who is so quiet even now that you feel the urge to wake him up.

Too bad Sras was transferred, he thinks. But at some point her foot slipped. And her hand. When Cremp tried to use the staff again. The whole thing started with a not unsightly brawl and ended in one of the illegal bars, arm in arm, before the brawl continued (only not against each other).

'Peace,' comes through a mixture of guitar riff and jetplane take-off on an aircraft carrier, 'is only in you. Only within you can you find it. You think it's dependent on the environment? Then you're wrong. And become a pawn.'

When sweats. And gets upset that he's sweating. And about the fact that he's upset. He used to know what calm was. In another life, far away from the noises, these terrible noises that cut through his head like sabres.

Yet he has made such good progress. He found peace on the tarmac. On the Marienplatz with all the tourists, the impressions. Even when they were downright tortured, with old recordings of the TV garden, the Tagesschau and Bundestag sessions when the Reichstag was still standing, downright attacks on taste, decency and truth, he had found peace. But now?

Where are you? If you are inside me, why don't I feel you? Where have I lost you?

'There are people who become restless when a door is slammed firmly shut. When they are slowly driven to anger because a child keeps asking.'

'Others remain calm, even in the face of noise, insults, untruths and threats.' Cremp pauses for a moment, looks along the walls where some statues of their saints are standing or sitting. 'Even when their insides are in turmoil, they remain calm. Even when there seems to be nothing else, they remain calm.'

Nothing else seemed to exist. Is there anything else besides this fear, deep fear, coming from the millennia, of the noise, When wonders? Of the twitching of the lightning, the earthquakes, all still misunderstood in the past. And today? The constant monotonous whine of the machines, the background noise of all the opinions, the conversations ...

'I know it's hard. And it can get harder and harder. If I had found a teacher before the revolution who could calmly answer questions from a bunch of children, I would have given him a medal. If I had found a politician who remained calm, even in the noise of his own self-centredness, I would have made him king of the world.'

Cremp walks between them.

'I know it's hard,' he repeats, 'but you, our elite, you have to get through it. Your ego will always find a reason to be restless. Whether it's that annoying neighbour or someone pulling a knife out in front of you. Or this music.' He turns the knob down.

When relaxes. Goldilocks has toughened up and seems to have found a certain calm. Others breathe a sigh of relief just like When, only the Japanese guy seems to have fallen asleep for good.

'But just as there will always be a reason to let restlessness control you, there will always be a place within you where you will find your peace and strength. Find that place! Then lose it. Then find it again, familiarise yourself with it. Embrace it until the drop has become a sea.'

A sea of silence.

Suddenly When feels the gentle wind on his skin, the sound of the ocean. He thinks back to the only time they were at the ocean together. The silence.

'You have to find the silence. Stay calm like a block of ice - even when the world around you is collapsing under the noise. Because restlessness leads to aversion, aversion leads to fear, and fear leads to anger.' Cremp switches off the noise completely.

When takes a deep breath.

'And our goal, peace, becomes unattainable.' Cremp's gaze glides over his pupils. It is unrecognisable what he feels. Maybe confidence. Or disappointment. 'The test is in a week's time. Anyone who doesn't pass is still welcome, of course.' Now he smiles encouragingly again, almost as if he regrets his role.

The tank.

The older models looked more like something out of an SF film, a failed attempt to build something special with all the poles and oxygen tanks. The good thing was that passers-by only thought it a building site.

The black tube, which is now just out of sight of the mob, is streamlined, something between a torpedo and a ski rack. There are no more oxygen bottles, nor is there a control panel. One because he wants to be on his own. The other because he no longer breathes as much as he used to.

'Everything is prepared. No immanent threats.'

His brother opens the tank, then hands him a small capsule.

When's body bows. He himself has already submerged and can only hear his voice from a distance. 'How far to the crowd?'

'Twenty metres.'

When nods.

Climbing a mountain at five thousand metres is fun, he thinks. Carrying a crate of stones up to the summit is a challenge.

'But the worst thing is their symbol.'

Everything becomes a mist as he slides into the water and puts the capsule in his mouth.

'Our beloved Melianne!'

Submerges.

'Perverted, stained with symbols of paganism!'

And sinks.

'Third step: the moment.'

Nearly all of them had quit; within one step. No, not quit. The Japanese man really turned out to be a child prodigy, went back to Japan and now runs a training centre there. Or is head of state. Or the incarnation of Kannon Ji - When's Japanese is a bit rusty.

Sras joined the Sisters of the Hand, which seemed only natural. On her first day there, she beat up two masters so badly that, coincidentally, two battlemaster positions became vacant that day. She accepted one of them.

His mate got bored with the silence and switched to the Observers, a kind of journalist, only without the greed, contempt for humanity and stupidity that has prevailed in ninety-nine per cent of the press over the last decade. At least that's the plan.

And now it's just the two of them.

Goldilocks - or rather Tara - has become so stone-cold quiet since the first few hours that she doesn't even have to go into meditation pose to immerse an entire building in silence. A sinister development, you might think. But then you catch a glimpse of her icy grey eyes, and a gentle smile from her caresses your soul. She will make it. No matter how many more steps and trials there are.

But When? His bonus of being the brother and having a special talent no longer matters. In the highest spheres, it's no longer talent that counts, but training. Perseverance. A goal that is worth it.

Does he have all that? Yes, he decides.

He practised his posture until it seemed unnatural not to sit, walk or stand upright. He has found and lost his peace and found it again, after countless hours in busy, noisy places, while looking for people who didn't leave a good mark on him. And listening to heavy metal and pop songs from the last few decades.

Now nothing stirs in him anymore. A still lake at night. No wind, not even the moon is reflected in the water.

You led me there. Now the only thing that disturbs the silence is the thought deep down that I won't surface again.

'There is only one time when you can meditate. And that is always now.' The veteran - calmer, somehow more understanding in recent weeks - shakes his head thoughtfully. 'Yes, I know. The oft-cited moment. The mysterious now. To be found in every esoteric book or proclamation of salvation. In every religion. Even our beloved Mr. Tolle would have named his firstborn this way if he had had the chance. But this time, and not for the first time, the truth is hiding right behind a banal façade.'

He gazes calmly out into the rain at the walls of Fürstenried Palace.

Has it actually not been raining since I started training? asks When. Or do I always wake up just in time for the next downpour? Is my mind always looking for the weather that suits it best?

'And how the moment is wasted. There's always a next time: 'I'll be better prepared tomorrow'. Or: 'I've achieved enough for today'. Does that sound familiar?' Without waiting for an answer, he continues: 'And how the moment has been trivialised. A life of mindfulness, how fruitful. How rich. But take my word for it.' His gaze wanders over When, then over Tara. 'The moment is everything. It's our gateway to ultimate wisdom. Our salvation. We just have to give it everything.'

The moment.

The salvation.

Yes. I could live with that goal.

'Immerse yourself in the moment. And stay there until you take your last breath. Or exist no longer.'

'And if we have to go to the toilet?' When's friend would have asked. And the veteran would have humourlessly held a catheter in the air, along with one or two disturbing devices.

'There are no disturbing noises, no thoughts that aren't in the moment. They are the only thing that feels real. Not the visualisations, not the deities or mantras. There is only reality. Observe it. Don't run away. Don't change it. Stay calm.' Now Cremp sits down and remains silent. 'Questions?' comes a low humming from his throat.

'What if the moment isn't beautiful?'

The veteran takes a deep breath.

Tara has already disappeared into the depths, When can tell by the room temperature.

'Then, my boy,' the veteran replies with a smile, 'the moment is not beautiful.'

When drops into a cross-legged position next to the speaker. He dries his hair with a handkerchief-sized towel and looks out over the deserted square. Empty beer cups are still lying around. They have also left their sticks and stones behind.

'They just left. Just like that.' The Tribune looks incredulous. Even his sound technicians have disappeared, and only a body-guard has remained. He is frantically holding a pepper spray.

Interesting. You want to fight, but you don't know what against.

'Brother.' When presses the radio. 'Get our big, bald friend a glass of water. Take his spray off, then drive him home.' He looks in the giant baby's direction again. 'And watch him. He's got potential.'

'You did this,' the tracksuit states.

'Yes.' replies the half-naked When.

'Like her back then? Is that how she saved us?'

When smiles weakly. 'Yes. And no. The goal is the same. But she used real power. I'm just a child against her.' He stands up and holds out a hand to the Tribune.

'Where did the people go? How...?'

'Answers. I said goodbye to them a long time ago. Perhaps the people have realised that hatred is the wrong path. Maybe they've remembered that someone is waiting for them at home.

That there is someone they need to look after. Grandparents
who need to be cared for. Partners who want to be respected.'
He smiles, his hand still open. 'Children we have to look after.
Even if we force them to stay seated.'

'Even if it's only thirty minutes a week,' he adds.

The man remembers the words. Maybe because they are his
own. 'No tricks?'

'No.'

Then the speaker grabs his hand, pulls himself up and looks
When deeply in the eye. A tiger that has been cornered.

'It's not over yet.'

His hand closes tighter. Until for a moment there is balance.
Pressure and counter-pressure. Hardness, softness.

'It never is.'

He nods, turns round and takes a few steps. Across the posters.
Then he pauses, speaks quietly to himself, yet it's impossible
for When not to hear. 'You may have manipulated them with
your mumbo-jumbo. Because they are simple. Unconscious.'
He smiles. 'But it didn't even tickle me ... No, wait, I'm lying.
And you don't deserve that. You're always so honest.'

He looks at him mockingly.

'I was quiet for a second. Peaceful. All pink. Like your whole
gay organisation.' His face contorts in disgust. 'Compassion.
Trust.'

He has finally regained his former strength. Is the Tribune of
endless political battles. And storms off.

'One second, Flipper. That's all,' he echoes.

When is alone. Smiles at the nickname the press gave him because of the tanks. Then he takes a bow.

Sorry to disappoint you, friend. You were too far away, too full
of energy. I didn't even include you for a tenth of a second.
The compassion you felt, is entirely your fault.

The briefing

'Friend, you look like you need a ride.' When dismounts, briefly checks the battery.

A little old man scowls at him. 'What do you mean? Do I look that old to you?'

When raises his hands apologetically. 'Quite the opposite.' He puts the handlebars in the old man´s doddering hands. 'Go in peace.'

'If you say so,' snaps the old man, turning to a passer-by. 'Hey you, the brother here has one e-bike too many. Interested?'

When smiles, turns and looks up. At her. In deep contemplation. And even then, her eyes radiate an infinite kindness.

He bows deeply, then walks deliberately up the steps to the head office and enters the reception room. Some of those present turn round and cast him appreciative glances. He nods back in a friendly manner.

'Activation?' Little Brother vibrates on his wrist.

'No. I like the human contact.'

'Mean. You know how I like to network with the central computer.'

Interesting, he thinks. The colder we get, the more emotional the robots become. Hopefully one day there will be a heroic machine to protect them from us humans.

'Welcome, brother.'

When bows to his sister. What power is at work in this place. And what power she possesses.

'I hope there was no trouble with our gatekeeper?' She smiles at him, somewhere from above, because she towers over When by two heads.

'No. I've known him for a long time. Unfortunately, he always forgets that.' Or at least he pretends to.

'Yes. But he's so sweet. And he'll outlive us all.'

'I'm sure he will.'

Her LB vibrates. She nods imperceptibly. 'You're already expected. First floor. I'll take you there.' She looks down at him. 'If you want to freshen up first, there are bathrooms. And I'm sure there's a uniform in your size.'

He is confused. Then he remembers that his skin hasn't seen water since the tank. Well, and the water in the tank is salty and a bit ... special.

'No, thank you very much. We'd better not keep him waiting.'

She beams at him. 'Wise decision, brother.'

He smiles a little sheepishly. 'Sometimes there's no turning back. Then you can only hope that wisdom wins again at the end of folly.'

Now she laughs out loud. Bright as a bell. 'One of his quotes. He'll love that!' She turns round and strides forward.

Yes, his quotes have often been useful.

The meeting room.

He hadn't been here for a long time. The last time was when some guardians had to settle a dispute between peasants. Tough fare. Since then, there's only been news for his Little Brother, then straight to the water tank, which hopefully meant a peaceful solution, and he wonders whether peacekeepers themselves will be able to enjoy peace at some point; and why the hall is empty, except for him.

'Your last mission was a success, I hear? Despite the ... delay?'

That voice.

'Yes. We were able to calm the crowd. All good people. Got a bit off track.' When turns round. 'As for the delay ... There were problems with the tank. The water wasn't the right temperature.'

17

An obvious lie is sometimes more honest than the truth. And more amusing.

The veteran looks at him doubtfully for a moment, then smiles. He has hardly changed. Maybe more muscle.

'Greetings, brother. I hope the room temperature here is comfortable for you.'

The strongroom, as tall as he is broad, bows. New robe, sleeveless, custom-made. Full grey hair, despite his ... How old is he? Two hundred?, When thinks.

He returns the greeting. 'Yes, very pleasant. Teacher.'

'Please...' Cremp laughs so heartily that it's infectious. 'That was a long time ago. But enough of the empty phrases, otherwise you and I will be sitting together for hours counting the grey hairs I got because of your ... creative moments.'

Determined, he strides past When and heads for a desk. There, Cremp pulls Little Brother off his arm. No, little is an understatement, this must be a luxury version. And When didn't even know there were variations.

Carefully positioning it on the table, Cremp whispers a command, then a light flares up.

'Today, my friend, you will get your first grey hair. Please forgive me in advance.'

When takes a deep breath. Lets the images pass by.

I have meditated in the strangest places and found peace. Not always immediately, and not always, but eventually. And it got better over time.

But put me in a classroom, having someone pacing up and down and ranting about a subject, and I'm as quiet as a swarm of bees ...must be karma.... and if he doesn't get to the point soon, I can't resist the urge to secretly shoot him with paper bullets. Not that I'd hit him ...

18

'This Confederation of cities includes some, surprisingly, cities, that declared independence during the upheaval. The armed forces of the former German army established a demilitarised zone around the area. Since then, they have tended to keep to themselves. A few visits, a few skirmishes, but not an important factor for us and our goal.' Cremp looks at him sharply. 'That's changed now.'

Cremp starts a visual recording. Not low-tech, more like a advertisement. High resolution shots that suggest camera equipment and cranes in the background.

Some people, the important ones, cavort around a central figure who seems to be EVEN more important. But the main character is someone else. Or rather: something else.

The crowd divides, revealing a glimpse of something that they are fawning over like sinners once did over the golden calf. But this is colourless. Metallic. Round. Ugly.

'May I introduce? Nuclear bomb. Older model. Not old enough, unfortunately.'

When is silent for a moment. Memories come back. Of her. Of the Night of the Candles.

'How did they get it?'

Cremp frowns.

'We don't know that. Maybe through allies. Perhaps stolen from some secret arsenal. How they got through the blockades is also a mystery to us. Worst case scenario ...'

A disguised aid transport, When finishes the sentence. And in the very worst case, one of ours.

'What do they want to do with it?'

'Nothing special at the moment. Boasting, intimidating, calling in a favour or two.' He pauses. 'But it won't stop there.'

No. When there's a bomb, there's always someone who will

press the button.

Russian crooks who played with the suitcase while drunk on vodka. And who knows how many American presidents and generals who would have loved to kick the nuclear football into the end zone.

More images flash up every second. These ugly weapons. Greedy for destruction. Submissive, caressing, just to be used.

The veteran becomes serious. When has never seen him like this before.

'Others will arm. The former Bundeswehr already had their fighters in the air before the bomb. No telling what's going on in their heads now. The Blokes will try to acquire the thing, elegant as ever, of course. Other clans will probably want it too. So do organisations with far less wise leaders. It's almost lucky she ended up with the Gaffeln. But only almost.'

Cremp calms himself, puts on a fighting face again. For the morale of the troops.

'If I know Grandad Toupet, he'll unscrew it and feed it into one of his ailing nuclear power plants.'

They both smile.

'Or put his hair on its head and have her represent him in the Elysee,' When continues the thought.

'Yes, what a gain in quality that would be.'

'There will be a meeting.'

A brother comes in and brings them tea.

'Tempers are still cool enough for a bit of diplomacy. Or rather sabre-rattling. This is our chance.' Cremp reaches for his cup and takes a sip.

'And who requested us?'

This time his smile seems a little forced. 'Yes, that's one of the rather complicated points. Unfortunately, we weren't invited.'

'I understand. That's...' When hesitates, 'something new.'

'Isn't it? And that's what makes the plan so attractive.'

There it is again, the old enthusiasm when he played tricks on the other masters.

'If my memory serves me right, you and your friend are the only ones who ever made it past the guards to the ceremony.'

When remembers his brothers' resistance. The first time he became inconspicuous. The headache the next day.

'The door just happened to be open.'

The veteran smiles. 'Yes, that happens. And our elite guards weren't really on their game that day either.'

Cremp plays lost in thought. 'Let's not hold that against them.'

Cremp nods. 'And how was it at Neuschwanstein?'

When wants to answer, but the veteran shakes his head.

'Please. The international incident was hardly worth mentioning, after all, you're her brother. And you had a reason.'

A reason. Yes. Jet black hair. I saw her then. For the first time.

'So, what do you think?'

When wakes from his thoughts.

The veteran looks at him questioningly. 'Ready to mix up another party? This time officially unofficial?'

'Yes.'

'Very good. You're accompanying an aid transport. We've negotiated free passage to the zone. A delegation will receive you. Our contact person will be waiting for you in the city. Everything else later.' Satisfied, his teacher switches off Little Brother. 'A briefing like this makes you hungrier than morning exercise with Master Ajun, and she does twenty kilometres every morning. Fancy the canteen? It's the turn of our exchange trainees from Nepal. They're serving Dal Bhat.'

'What exactly is my job?' asks When twenty Danjavaaht and

thirty sweats later.

The veteran smiles at a Nepalese woman in a sari. 'As always: peace. We're supposed to bring the bomb home, dismantle it and shoot it into space where it can't hurt anyone. The second goal? Everyone should fall into each other's arms and love each other.' He looks around absently. 'A kingdom for a nice beer,' he murmurs wistfully.

When smiles. You've got a few knaves in your past too, haven't you?

'And if it all doesn't work out?'

Cremp becomes more serious. Focuses on him like an eagle on a mouse. 'Then survive. And get home in one piece.'

So that's it, it goes through his head. Not a rally. Not a brawl he has to settle, but an emergency. Human lives are at stake.

And not for the first time, he is afraid of the lack of fear in him. Of the calm.

'Where will the meeting take place?'

'We don't know. The city has undergone many changes since the takeover. We assume that the conditions ... won't be ideal.'

'So probably no meditation music, ringing bowls and incense sticks?'

'Not likely.' Cremp smiles.

A new environment. People are extremely dismissive - as his other instructors have always jokingly put it. And no water tank. The mountain. The rocks. This time in the death zone.

'Who will be attending the meeting?'

'We have confirmation of the Council Chairman and his advisors. Some Englishmen. Also some of the remaining Americans. Quite manageable, actually, but our analyses show a different picture.' He takes an imperceptible breath, as if he has something to confess. 'Other possible participants are hostile clans from the east. Allies from the other free cities. Small war-lords who want to make themselves important. Perhaps one or two small superpowers who want to have their say. And there will certainly be no shortage of rich and beautiful people on this occasion.'

No smile. Sarcasm doesn't look good on you, brother. The last comment wasn't meant as a joke; it was a warning.

'It won't be easy, but you've dealt with the Tribune. And with the peasants. What's a councillor and some of the most power-ful people on this continent compared to that?'

Silence.

'Brother, I don't have to tell you ...'

What's at stake ... yes, that's what they used to call it.

' ...what the consequences of your mission's success might be.'

No, but something in him wants to hear them anyway, the beautiful consequences. Peace. Friendship. Our path that is car-ried out into the world.

'And what happens if the mission fails.'

No. It's been said too often.

Can we actually exist without negative consequences? Or them without us? The apocalyptic horsemen who are not far away, who have always been among us?

Hatred. Enmity. Death. And our path spurned by the world. Useless.

Cremp takes a break.

When was nervous. Before this meeting. And he is now. 'No. I will fulfil the task,' he says, his voice firm.

'We all believe that.' The veteran rises. 'So, it's time to report back to our saints. And tell them about your extraordinary wil-lingness and motivation ... They'll be pleased.'

'I'm glad to hear that.'

'Any more questions?'

'Are you coming with me, Master? That sounds like an adven-ture for you.'

Cremp seems to consider the matter for a millisecond, then laughs. 'My humble self? No. I'm an instructor, I've done my tours of duty. If the armed forces wave you through, think of me. It was a tough struggle,' he adds modestly. 'Besides, I have children. With a wife who doesn't find me quite as annoying as the rest of the world. No, I have my battles to fight here.'

'I understand. When will I be transferred?'

The veteran looks sharply at the old-fashioned clock on the wall and does the maths. Quite a long time, When thinks, for a former soldier.

Then Cremp nods in satisfaction. 'That's entirely up to you. Right now or in an hour, if you want to say goodbye first.' He grins mischievously. 'But you Guardians so rarely stick to things, I hear.'

'That's true. An hour would still be ... pleasant.'

'That's a deal. I'll get everything ready. Quasimodo has been informed and the plane is already waiting for you at the ABF. You'll also meet your team there.'

'My team?'

'Brother...' He looks at When sympathetically. Like a father tending to his son's wound. 'Do you really think we'd let you go alone? Then you're more arrogant than I thought.' He smiles.

When bows, then both men shake hands.

'Master, please don't tell me now that this is exactly what I was trained for.'

'No, don't worry. No one has ever been trained for this, my dear boy.'

U29

He takes a look back. The Fürstenried Castle. Probably the most inconspicuous in the history of Bavaria, between the A95 motorway in the direction of Garmisch, and the Waldfriedhof, where all the candles had first started to burn that night.

When carefully adjusts his uniform and breathes in the fresh morning air. As he passes, he greets the street sweeper, who he knows doesn't even work for the city, which makes When admire his hard work all the more. Then he walks towards Schweizer Platz and enters the underground station on underground line 3.

Orange, he thinks with a smile. If it isn't destiny.

Six o'clock in the morning.

It has taken a little longer to let go of his attachments. The train is almost empty, with just one elderly lady sitting cross-legged like him - the seats now support this sitting position. A sister from the Order of the Hand politely gives him a wai.

The underground trains have become silent, the underground drivers friendly robots. Only for tourists have some been programmed into a grumpy mode, for old times' sake. But they are polyglot and he has to smile at the way Forstenrieder Allee sounds in Chinese. And in Hindi.

Brudermühlstraße.

A group of elderly ladies and gentlemen enter. Apparently regional tourists visiting the capital. Heavy Bavarian accent, Tegernsee region, he guesses. He stands up politely and offers his seat to a lady who, at probably a hundred years old, looks so delicate and fragile that a breeze could blow her away.

'Young Mo,' says the lady, looking at him with eyes that could cut through a tightrope. 'Do I look like I want to sit down?'

'Of course not,' says When apologetically and sits back down to the laughter of her friends.

'That's right. Always save energy, you don't have that much, you young things!' Then she gives him a hidden look of gratitude. For knowing how she would react and getting up anyway.

Politeness can sometimes be complicated, he thinks as he marvels at the beauty of these old people.

Implerstraße, and When gets on the U29. He is underground and a part of him finds it still weird. But he can feel the power vibrating above him. On the Theresienwiese, the new home of his order. The home of his brothers and sisters.

He remembers the early thirties. Was it her aura that made the air vibrate with compassion and saturated the ground with wisdom so strong that it was unrivalled in the history of mankind? Or was it the soul of this corner of the world, the magic of the mountains? Or, in the end, the hitherto hidden depths of the Bavarian soul? There was much puzzlement around the world, except in Bavaria itself.

Many politicians and business leaders back then voluntarily resigned from office during the time of upheaval, went into seclusion or joined his order. New institutions such as the Council of the Wise were founded and the Research Centre for Peaceful Technology was established. And the country was given a new name: Awaria.

26

New laws were created for peace.

But the strange thing was that their society developed almost entirely without rules. So strong had the dream been, so great her sacrifice, so deep the wisdom given to each person that night, that people realised how precious every moment is. That our universe is at stake whenever you slam the door in someone's face. Or helpfully hold it open.

He only entered the stage later, when much had already been built, set up and established. When he finally realised that it was his sister who had snatched the planet from the jaws of death. At the last moment, he realised his future fate so quickly that he fled, never to be found.

But then came the pleas. The rest of Germany was falling apart at the time, the world was in flames and the young Free State was fighting for its recognition, for its survival. The newly formed academy, with all its capable teachers from all areas of devotion and meditation, with all its noble aims, needed students who would master the spirit. They were to prove that peace is more powerful than all weapons and all anger. So he, the brother of Saint Melianne, became one of them.

The U29 - pink like his first meditation cushion and only completed a few years ago - is getting fuller.

The lights are on, mainly for people who don't live in Munich. School classes are now mingling with Friends going about their work and members of his order heading for the various buildings of the Entschweren Akademie. Everyone is laughing, he remarks with a smile, even the accountants. This is despite the fact that they have to recalculate and check the value of many people's money every day since the introduction of the secure money system.

The students are smiling too, probably since the unannounced tests have been abolished and teachers are getting the best possible meditation training. His sisters and brothers smile anyway, which has often earned Awaria the name 'Land of the Silly Grin', of course from people who have lost their laughter.

Goetheplatz.

When found the old man's literature fascinating, at least from the time he was forced to read it. Sometimes exaggerated like all romantics, he had thought, just like Goethe did think of himself later on.

Then he had fallen in love at the age of eighty(Goethe, that is), and When himself did as well, and so The Sorrows of Young Werther no longer seemed so far-fetched to him.

What a pity that they could never enjoy the gift of meditation, he thinks and takes a moment full of compassion for all those people.

Then suddenly a little boy and a little girl stand in front of him and just stare.

'You're When, aren't you?' the girl asks in a bright voice. Esperanto Square. Then the main railway station. A city in itself, underground, now full of small libraries, meditation rooms, archives and clothing shops for those who still value it. And of course there are the ubicuitous bakeries everywhere with their nationally renowned baguettes and sandwiches, all in nine different flavours.

'That's true,' says When too quietly, which he finds suspicious.

The people to his right and left look at him, but only smile mildly.

'And your names are?' he asks, bowing his head respectfully

in greeting.

The rest of the group of children, apparently on an excursion, have taken their seats. Some of them seem to be meditating or sleeping, both of which he likes. The two carers - nurses from the education department - look at him a little apprehensively, but he smiles back reassuringly.

'I'm Pleni and this is Floryan,' says the girl before the boy can reply.

'Pleased to meet you, Pleni and Floryan.'

'Your sister was so beautiful,' the girl says suddenly, more shy this time.

Floryan just nods, deep in thought.

'I have a picture of her.' She opens an inconspicuous locket attached to her necklace and hands it to him.

'She was,' says When as he silently looks at the picture of his sister. An original, he realises, one of the few. Not an exaggerated copy, like the ones that came into circulation after the upheaval.

'Do you miss her?' the boy asks gently, earning a scowl from Pleni, who suddenly finds this question too private.

When smiles. 'Yes and no.' No lectures now, he tells himself. Just the truth. 'Sometimes when I'm sad, I wish I could go back and talk to her. Then I find peace and remember her. And realise that she never really left,' he says more to himself, and wonders how true that is. Or how true he feels it is.

Slowly, more and more children gather around him, and the adults have also started to switch off their LBs and listen. Once again, one of the sisters looks at him, asking him with her eyes if she should intervene.

No, thinks When. We can't choose our role, his instructor always said. But we can make the best of it.

'You have a silver star, don't you?' he asks Pleni, pointing to a badge on her collar.

'Yes,' she says proudly. 'I can meditate for half an hour.'

'That's really very good,' replies When appreciatively. 'I couldn't do that at your age.' Which is true, but he smiles to himself when he realises that she immediately believes him.

'Floryan can't do that either,' she says almost regretfully. 'He always thinks about playing.'

When smiles first at Pleni, then at the boy. 'Everyone has their own pace. And you can also meditate while playing,' he says with a smile.

Then he folds his legs into halflotus. His brothers and sisters around him nod and do the same. Some of them do it from a standing position and so quickly that his knees almost start to hurt as he watches.

'Would you do me the honour?' he asks into the car and the teachers give him a brief nod.

'Children, commando pretzel.'

And like a gentle wave, each child glides into the meditation pose, some into the cross-legged position, some into the warrior pose, others glide their hand over their face, one pupil has a rosary in her hand.

Almost synchronised, they close their eyes together with When.

And begin to breathe.

Pinakotheken.

The children respectfully said goodbye to him.

Pleni wanted to give him her star as a gift, and he can't remember the last time he blushed like that.

She had looked puzzled, and When realised that his sacred memory was already crumbling.

That's all right. As soon as you put yourself on a pedestal, you've already lost touch with the ground.

Floryan had pulled her along with him, preventing any more

awkward questions, and When had smiled gratefully at him. The two sisters also smiled happily before getting out with their protégés to admire the museums.

How different people have become, he muses as the underground stops at Elisabethplatz. In the past, you couldn't get a child past the sweets at the supermarket checkout without shouting.

I know it...I was one of those kids.

And the ability to disengage from a screen became so low in the late twenties that studies had shown serious attention deficits. As if the sharp increase in accidents caused by smartphone users and the growing brutalisation weren't clear enough.

And guilty again, he thinks, remembering his time as an orphan, a gambler, a thief, a refugee.

What would have become of us, sister, if it hadn't been for you?

Münchner Freiheit.

Many of the names have remained because Munich's proud past was not to be touched, mistakes of history were not to be repeated and what belongs to its history, its soul, was not to be erased.

And yet, so much has changed, he thinks as the U29 passes Dietlindenstraße, then Alte Heide. And so much had changed to the worse, according to the opposition.

Is that true, he asks himself quietly? Do you have to be strong to survive in this world? Do the strong have to be intelligent and the intelligent have to be strong, as Kästner demanded?

Yes, the Council also decided when it made unpopular decisions. Like the development of Quasimodo, the authorisation of genetically modified grain or the establishment of the Order of the Hand.

Is it even possible to find peace in this world and still be strong enough? To find the balance between compassion and coldness?

When thinks of the people, of the school class, of his friends. Of Melianne.

Slowly, the final stop comes into view. The arena, meeting place of the world's largest meditation sit-ins, next to the new research centre, the origin of some of the greatest inventions the world has ever seen.

The scientists have done their job, he thinks, and do it every day.

We Guardians must now fulfil our task.

You have proven to us, sister, that love is stronger than all the destructiveness in the world.

I will not let you down.

Green meadows

How quiet the airport has become, When thinks, throws his bag over his shoulder and takes a deep breath.

The technology centre had been as breathtaking as ever. An army of people in white coats, certainly as polite as anyone in the country, but unfortunately just too busy, too lost in thought, to have time for politeness. They scrutinised him attentively, more as a research object that they would like to study and put under a microscope.

The director had invited him to a meal, which he had to decline with thanks, as time was pressing.

'What a pity,' the lady had said modestly, as if it wasn't him or anyone else in the world who should regret not sitting at a table with Ricarda Hoyle-Fraunhofer.

We are not of this world, his masters have always said. But we live in it. And we have to give it everything we've got to have a chance. If the Academy is the heart of Awaria, then the Technology Centre is the head. If it alone controls us, life becomes hollow and bleak. But if we don't have our heads, we may never get the chance to develop our hearts.

Yes, When thinks, and remembers the bright, intelligent eyes of this lady. She is the inventor of the EMP field, developer of the LBs, the super seeds. She and her team are responsible for Awaria surviving the upheaval.

Lost in thought, he boards a small shuttle bus - with innovative hydrogen technology, of course - to take him to the centre of the airport.

How clean the air is here.

It's almost a shame. As a child, he loved the smell of aeroplanes. And the roar of the turbines.

He never flew, but he was fascinated by Munich Airport back then. And certain financial opportunities of course if you only travelled without paying on the S1 or S8 to save costs.

He steps out onto the open space and looks up at the huge roof above him. The tower, which since reunification has only had to direct gliders and airships, rises above him like a giant water reservoir.

Curious as he was back then, he strolls across the square, observing the people as unobtrusively as possible. There is no hustle and bustle. Not even among the citizens. But most of those present are sisters and brothers from the Alliance of Silence from all over the world. Smiling, a little exhausted from the journey, which has become quite long and arduous again.

And worthwhile, the masters would now say.

Many greet him and bow their heads. Did they recognise him? Hopefully not.

The kerosene is gone, he suddenly realises. Replaced by friendship, affection. What seemed strange before has finally grown together.

He suddenly notices guides from his order everywhere, recognisable by their white armbands, helping visitors. Green is everywhere. Meditation forms with different themes for those who want to keep their faith can be seen everywhere, and prayer rooms can also be found from time to time.

'No more controls. No passport checks. No policemen,' his little brother vibrates. 'If the former ministers of the interior had realised that back then, it would have been the end of them.'

'You're a rebel today,' notes When. 'Do you think it's a shame that parties no longer exist? Because you can no longer demonstrate against them? Together with your other robot mates?'

'Excuse me. But it must be my programming. And my programmer. She was one of the first of the zero hour.'

When smiles. 'And I think she was a bit radical.'

'That word is far too harsh. After all, there was no bloodshed, was there?'

In his imagination, the LB crosses his virtual arms in front of his chest.

'And the result is something to be proud of.'

When looks around. Closes his eyes for a moment. And feels the waves. A group of children in meditation. A brother in a splendid Senegalese costume showing two Valhall guards the way.

'Yes. Yes, it is.'

He walks on slowly.

Foreign colours and smells waft into his nose, competing with the food stalls, which in turn fight for the noses of potential customers.

And then he suddenly finds himself in front of the only airport brewery in the world. It has survived the outbreak of war and the energy revolution unscathed: the Airbräu.

'Dear friend, please. That's the rule,' he hears someone say.

When briefly considers whether he should use his LB to locate him. But that no longer seems necessary.

'How many times do you want me to repeat it, my dear friend? My device doesn't have this function.'

When follows the words and catches sight of two desperate-looking waitresses in pretty dirndls talking to a customer.

A fine suit, tailor-made, even if it's hard for When to imagine. He has combed back his full black hair as if he were about to abolish compulsory military service. Healthy skin colour and a conciliatory smile on his lips that could almost make even When want to sign over all his possessions to the man immediately, if he had any.

'Dear friends. Please sit down, and let's talk about this.'

When follows the conversation with interest. He notices how the voices become quieter, almost inaudible. How the smile of the man in the suit becomes softer and softer. How the waitresses' facial features relax more and more until only a smile remains.

And another order.

No meditation, but the man controls the energies, wonders When and remembers.

'Two will accompany you. The less, the merrier. In this case. The rest of the aid transport is already on its way.' The veteran turns back to his LB. 'They were carefully selected. They're the best in their field. Just like you. Open the file.'

Images are projected onto the wall. A man in his early forties appears. Black hair, casual white shirt, a yacht behind him.

'Yes. He's not a brother of ours. If that's what you're wondering.'

When nods. Obviously not.

'His name is Latour. Degrees in political science and diplomacy from various universities. Worked for many organisations after the upheaval. One hundred per cent success rate. Knows God and the world, rich and poor, and very poor and very rich.' He pauses for a moment. 'He does the actual negotiations. He knows our goals. With any luck, you won't even have to reach into your bag of tricks.' The veteran smiles at him encouragingly.

'That would be nice,' replies When, almost sincerely.

'How did the connection come about?'

'Well, word of mouth. You know ... I know someone who knows someone whose friends might be able to help us.' He pauses. 'But your real question is, why is he helping us?'

'Yes. 'When nods.

'There are several reasons. An old debt, I think, a little profit. And a thirst for adventure probably isn't at the bottom of his list either.' The veteran fixates When. 'If you're asking me about his loyalty, I'd have to pass. The world out there has become chaotic to me. Without pattern. And so have their characters.'

'If the Council trusts him, so will I.'

'Good. Besides, our next choice would have been a foreign minister of the former FRG, in which case we might as well press the button ourselves.'

Satisfied, the man reaches for his glass, then suddenly leans towards When and looks directly at him. 'Can I be of any help? Er...' he hesitates briefly, 'brother?'

When is not surprised. He senses the man's attentiveness. However, the fact that When is still standing and staring in the middle of a beer garden doesn't make it particularly difficult.

'Yes. I'm looking for Mr. Latour. We have a journey together ahead of us.'

'Ah, that would be me.' He eyes When once more, then looks apologetic. 'Forgive me, please. And take a seat. I should have recognised you earlier.' He rises briefly and folds his hands in front of his chest.

A perfect Wai. He knows our customs, When thinks, and returns the greeting.

'Thank you.'

'It's an honour to meet her brother. Can I order you something? Vegetarian, I presume? The Obatzda here is very good. And don't worry, it's on me. And by me, of course, I mean your order.'

Without waiting for an answer, he calls one of his new favourite waitresses to the table, orders a portion of Obatzda and another beer.

'A nice little place, isn't it? Who would think that one of the most beautiful beer gardens in Munich could be found here in Halbergmoos? And one that sells meat?' His gaze wanders upwards, where a few white gliders are catapulted into the sky.

When's gaze falls on the empty wheat beer glasses standing neatly in a row in front of him. 'What was this little dispute about, if you don't mind me asking?'

Latour waves it off. 'Oh, not a dispute. More like an opportunity to make friends. In my humble opinion, the control your council has placed on alcohol consumption is a little too ... harsh. That's why I took the LB off.'

'And thus no way for him to inject the chemicals to combat the alcohol.'

'Yes. There's little point, I think, in drinking without listening to the soft words of alcohol.'

The order comes. Everything is served up carefully and with a smile, including a telephone number.

'And you have convinced them of your point of view?'

'Of course I did. That was amusing! Besides, the ladies and gentlemen here are just doing their job.' He smiles. 'Speaking of convincing. I guess that's why I'm here, isn't it?'

When looks at his beautifully arranged cheese balls garnished with parsley and studded with three salt sticks. He says a quick thank you and begins to eat. Finally he nods. 'Are you familiar with our mission?' he asks the diplomat.

'I've skimmed through the papers,' he replies, smiling nonchalantly.

And memorised everything within a minute, that smile wants to say, that much When has already understood.

'I was a little ... surprised at first. A Belgian who is supposed to mediate conflicts within Germany? Strange.'

You're not the only one who finds that strange, friend.

'But then I remembered that Germans and Belgians got along great for a long time. That is, until stupidity started to reign.' He takes a small sip of the beer. 'So it almost makes sense. Besides, I'm the best.'

No smile or affectation this time. He's firmly convinced. Good. We're going to need that confidence. When watches him more closely. But your vanity isn't the only reason you're taking this job. I can sense that.

'What about you, brother? What did you do to be let loose on the world beyond the screen?'

When smiles. I guess he'll have to get used to that kind of me-

38

taphor. 'Being Awarian, I guess. That's all,' he plays along and gets an appreciative smile from his counterpart.

Not that I could have chosen.

'Yes. Has advantages, and sometimes disadvantages. I've been there.' And for a brief moment Latour becomes thoughtful, orders the bill and gives a huge tip. 'When does our plane leave? Not that I'm looking forward to a flight in a better soapbox, but I guess you have to make sacrifices for peace.'

'That's probably the case.'

'But if no drinks are served, I'm out.'

When smiles, finishes his meal and activates Little Brother. 'The glider is ready. Apparently our launch has priority. A delegation from Tibet needs to see if their meditation is any good. We shouldn't put too much strain on their peace and serenity.'

The diplomat smiles adventurously. 'We shouldn't.' He reaches for a small briefcase and stands up. ' But isn't there a third participant? Any of your whipping squad?'

When stands up and thinks back. 'What about the third participant? '

The veteran had grinned.

'Be patient, my friend. Where's your joy for the unknown? Let yourself be surprised.' He laid a fatherly hand on When´s shoulder. 'Believe me. You won't be disappointed.'

When returns to the now. 'Yes. But knowing him, he's already waiting on the tarmac.

Him.

Or her.

Everywhere you look, you can still see the tarmac of the faded runways, you can feel the indentations left by hundreds of A380s.

When looks thoughtfully over the green area while a brother takes them to their aircraft.

Only a few position lights are flashing, as the ban on night flights has been extended. Stationary winches are waiting to take gliders aloft. Air cargo ships are wandering like tame clouds towards the horizon. And every now and then a snow-white glider or a Lilium jet takes off.

'The only thing missing here are grazing cows,' says the diplomat with a grin. 'I don't know how your state survives, but it ... has something.' He smiles. 'Something of a faery tale, of course. A very, very strange faery tale. But it has something.'

The brother carefully avoids the flight paths, Latour thinks to himself, should a plane land here once an hour.

'Brother, what if a real plane gets lost and has to make an emergency landing here? You're hardly going to intercept five hundred tons with gentle words.'

'Very unlikely, friend. Quasimodo wouldn't allow it. Unfortunately.' When looks regretful. 'But our friends from the Alliance have a small airport in Memmingen with the Council's permission. Since most planes can still glide about one hundred and seventy kilometres after the engines break down, that would be an option.'

'I see.' The diplomat adjusts his suit. Sweat appears on his forehead and his breathing quickens.

Have I deteriorated physically like this, he wonders? Or do these brothers just have a crazy pace as soon as they move?

'There's your aeroplane.'

Streamlined, with the word Neinhorn painted on the fuselage in blue letters. Two figures are standing behind the glider, one of which seems somehow ... disturbing to Latour.

That definitely doesn't look like on-board service, grumbles Latour inwardly, while he wishes he was wearing casual sportswear.

'I wish you a safe journey, my friend,' says the brother and bows to Latour.

He knows nothing of our mission. I can sense that.

Then he turns to When. 'Go in peace, brother.'

'Go in peace,' replies When, bowing low.

Latour looks briefly after the young brother, who has resumed his half-walking, half-running pace while greeting a group of Gelugpas who are wriggling their old bones out of one of the gliders. Latour turns away and gives When, whose eyes are already looking ahead, an encouraging pat on the shoulder.

'OK, where can I check in my luggage here now? Aha, and there's the pilot. And apparently also a co-pilot.' He gives a friendly nod to a man in uniform.

Well, man would be a bit of an exaggeration, more like a boy who looks sixteen. But he must be good at something, at least he's skilfully hooking up the tow rope, as far as Latour can tell.

'And here we have our stewardess.'

The second person. A woman. With a friendly smile and one hand outstretched, he approaches her.

And When's heart leaps.

It's her, it shoots through his head. At the same time, he feels a punch in the stomach.

Stewardess. Good thing you don't know, my worldly-wise friend, When thinks to himself with a certain secret satisfaction, how deeply you've just peered into the last light.

'Sawhadi krap?' Latour greets her in a friendly manner and looks at her.

Dark brown skin, large shining eyes that seem to fixate on something behind his skull.

Well, at least you had the right continent, When thinks, wondering about the diplomat's inaccuracy.

She stops just short of Latour, and When wonders if she's going to rip his outstretched hand right off and beat him up with it.

But she only smiles - that is, her lips curl in the remotest hint of a smile. Then she clasps the proffered hand. 'It's a pleasure, friend.' And the words aren't even drowned out by cries of pain.

She must have calmed down. How ironic, she never managed that in class.

Then she glides past the diplomat, a jaguar whose movements leave no trace, not even a breath of air.

And suddenly she is standing in front of him. 'Brother. It's a pleasure to see you again.'

She gives him a deep wai. But he is too distracted and can barely control himself not to take up a defensive position. To avoid taking the worst hits.

'Sister,' he says just in time, without seeming rude. 'Me too. It's been a long time.'

She smiles and he can finally relax a little.

The smell of the training room, of sweat and tears and the occasional drop of blood, leaves him.

'Yes. You must have passed the last test with honours, otherwise you wouldn't be here.'

He smiles guardedly. 'They let me pass. But it was close, I guess.'

'How wonderfully modest. So Marienplatz was luck too? How nice when luck is on our side like that.'

'Yes. But one of your units had already done some good groundwork, I heard. The people there were probably already so scared that I just had to turn on the valve.'

'Yes, my unit,' she smiles apologetically. 'We can go a little overboard sometimes.'

You were alone, it suddenly flashes through his mind. Your

Order never sends out more than two - and only when there's a war going on.

In the background, he notices the diplomat, who looks a little out of place for the first time since When met him.

'Sorry, friend, how rude of me.' When steps between his two new team-mates. 'Latour, may I present Sras Chann. Battlemaster of our order. She accompanies us. For our protection.'

Latour smiles at the delicate figure in front of him, and When knows exactly what is going on inside him. He almost expects the diplomat to want to hold the door of the glider open for her, if it had a real one.

'Pleased to meet you.'

'Chann, this is Eric Latour. He will be conducting the negotiations.'

She nods respectfully at him. 'Suasdey, bong bro,' she replies. When has to smile to himself. Gotcha, he thinks. Too soon, though.

'Chamreap suah, ong srey,' replies the diplomat in pure Khmer. Then he points in the direction of the glider, in which the pilot is already doing the final instrument check, using disturbing words such as Flautenschieber. 'We should be on our way. After all, the world won't save itself.'

A jolt goes through the, what could you call it ... airplane,' ponders When. He has taken a seat next to Latour in the narrow fuselage. Sras sits in front of him.

Then the winch slowly pulls up and the glider begins to roll roughly over the grass.

'That was a test, wasn't it?' When asks the diplomat, marvelling at the same time that he can still whisper secretively after all these years of boundless openness. 'You knew straight away that she was Khmer and not Thai. That was a provocation,

43

wasn't it?'

'Yes.' He looks at him seriously. 'There aren't many of us. I have to rely on everyone keeping a cool head, especially in enemy territory. After all, we're here to make peace.'

The glider speeds up, then suddenly everything feels easier as the pilot changes the angle of the wings.

'Besides, she can't beat them all up.' The diplomat watches her. Shouldn't she have weapons with her? At least some kind of ... stick?

She turns round at that moment, which he is sure is a coincidence, smiles and then looks at When, who has his eyes closed. 'Are you all right, brother?'

'I just realised I've never flown before,' When whispers as the glider gently loses contact with the ground.

Silence. Like in a tank. A flow. He takes a deep breath. The infinite space. And I am like a leaf in the wind.

And when he opens his eyes, he looks up into the blue sky. 'Everything's fine, sister. It's wonderful.'

She smiles, nods at him and looks ahead again.

'Altitude three hundred and fifty metres. Releasing the tow rope now,' says the pilot and looks around the small cabin, beaming with joy. 'We'll reach our cruising altitude in a few minutes. It looks like the weather is on our side. Blue skies all the way to our destination.'

All of a sudden, he descends a little, maybe not even ten metres, when a downdraft, When suspects between two heartbeats, or a hole in the thermic hits the machine and he realises that he's not quite in the flow yet.

'Don't worry. It's just the Isar and the Würm. They both have a long arm.'

The pilot pulls gently on the control stick. The glider calms down and slowly rises again.

Latour looks down. He sees endless fields in full ripeness.

The Morgenthau plan. If someone had ever predicted this to

the Allies, what feels like an infinite number of years ago, they would have laughed out loud. How things are different here compared to the rest of the world.

'We've reached our cruising altitude,' the pilot announces. 'If there's any more research to be done, you should fire up your little brothers again now.'

What kind of language, When thinks. Must be from the daily adrenaline.

'We'll meet Quasimodo in a few minutes. At that time anything with a circiut that isn't switched off will be worthless.'

Quasimodo

'One hundred and eighty seconds before hitting the shield.' The pilot quickly and precisely switches off all electronic items, even if there aren't many.

Sras only opens her eyes briefly, then closes them again. Only now does Latour realise that she has no LB.

Probably just a hindrance in combat, he thinks, switching off his hologram documents, then the computer.

'Little brother, you're getting a little time out now. We're approaching the border area of Awaria,' When whispers to the robot. 'You know what that means.'

Below them, the last foothills of Franconia fly by, with Aschaffenburg visible a little further ahead.

'Oh please, master.' The LB is far too emotional again, When realises. 'I can manage that. It's going to be a hot ride.'

'Yes. A very hot one.' When smiles and presses the off switch. Quasimodo. He doesn't know who came up with this name, but it must have been a Hugo lover, an admirer of Notre Dame.

'The nickname goes back to the hunchback's heroic defence of his beloved church. And that of his beloved Esmeralda,' says the pilot, as if he had read When's mind.

Against an opponent who was actually on his side, thinks Latour, who once wrote a work on Notre Dame de Paris. But he says nothing. A piece of wood against an army, he thinks, so the analogy is a bit misleading.

'The actual name is EMP 300X. Invented by HF, it is the world's first static EMP field,' the pilot continues.

The EMP field. The magic shield against all dragon fire, Latour thinks. The difference between your perfect world and the world outside.

'And it works how exactly? Forgive me for asking, but I'm curious.'

When smiles softly, the pilot almost bursts out laughing and even Sras smiles at the question.

Ah, thinks Latour, something that makes Team Order a little arrogant.

'Friend,' replies the pilot. 'I really can't tell you. All I know are rumours.'

And besides brother, you'd rather die than share the world's best-kept secret.

Latour looks at When, but he just smiles apologetically.

'I don't even know what's keeping this marvellous box in the air.'

The diplomat nods in understanding. 'And let me guess, master. You could tell me, but you'd have to kill me afterwards.'

'Yes, unfortunately.' She smiles disarmingly.

He smiles back, then looks out of the window.

'Ten more seconds,' the pilot announces. 'You are now leaving the Bavarian sector.'

Well, someone's been paying attention in class, Latour thinks. He looks at the sky, then at the ground. But, as on the entry, there is nothing to be seen. Except that this nothingness is protecting an entire nation.

Suddenly there is a short crack in his ear and they are through.

'Friends and brothers,' says the pilot almost solemnly.
'Welcome to the Federal Republic of Germany.'
He pauses. 'Or what's left of it.'

"What's that?" When looks up into the sky. And sees only iron.
 He's never been behind the shield before, the diplomat thinks.
What must that look like to him?

 "That, brother, is the rest of the world," says the pilot as he
switches on the few devices again.

 Iron in all shapes, some of them almost blocking out the sun,
the vibrations filling the air, making even his guts tremble imperceptibly.

 "Don't worry, brother," the pilot says with an understanding
smile. "We're far too low for us to collide with all that junk. Or
get sucked into a turbine."

 He slowly pushes the glider down, another hundred meters,
just to be on the safe side. Above them, wave after wave of aircraft ploughs through the sky, casting shadows on the inconspicuous glider.

 "But how can that be?" asks When, still fascinated and shaken
by the spectacle of kerosene and engines.

 "That they don't blow each other out of the sky? That happens
often enough," replies the pilot. "But there are sensors that usually prevent that. Some of these machines now even only fly by
AI."

 Sras is awake. If you can even call that sleep what the members of her order do when they close their eyes.

 "What our brother actually means, I think, is how the world
could go on like this." She hesitates. "After all that's happened." She doesn't look back, but When senses the questioning
undertone.

 He nods. "People have all seen the same things. Experienced

it."

That's not true, and you know it. People never experience the same thing, because the same thing doesn't exist.

"How can they just carry on as if nothing had happened?"

Suddenly, a fist hits the little glider from above as a plane as big as an aircraft carrier flies overhead at far too close a distance.

The pilot then drops his calm and swears quietly, apparently in Spanish. He is struggling to maintain control. He allows the loss of altitude and then carefully steers against it again until he has stabilized the plane. And When now knows how small their vehicle really is.

"The Global Near-Death Experience," the diplomat says absently as he looks after a streamliner carrying someone exclusive to the west.

"Humanity, in all its glory. As close to an exodus as we've ever seen," says Latour, almost to himself.

The pilot nods barely perceptible. Sras remains attentively silent.

"Similar to the near-death experience of a single person who has looked into the never-ending abyss of his own end. Stories about this are as old as humanity itself. And even if we dismiss 99.9 percent of them as frippery, 0.1 percent remain undeniable truth."

Even without your psychic abilities, the diplomat thinks, but doesn't say it.

"Apart from lights and helping spirits, demons and so on, it always remains an absolutely drastic experience. And usually results in radical changes of personality and actions." He fixes on a point on the horizon, perhaps a small moment without a steely shadow between him and the sun. "Only this time, no individual was affected." He pauses.

When realizes that Latour is in lecture mode.

"But nine billion people."

The Fall of the Wall. The Eleventh of September. People remember exactly where they were at that time.

Where was he, he asks himself, on that Christmas Eve in 2033? On the day, or rather the night, that changed everything?

'Everyone was looking into the abyss,' he continues.

And sees the sky in front of him again. He was sitting there with his mum, stuffed full of treats. Yes, it's not his holiday, but he's always liked Christmas. The scents. The food, the shining children's eyes. The shining stars. A night when everything looks good, at least once.

Or did.

Until a star appeared out of nowhere. And then a second one.

At first, many people thought it was a shooting star and rejoiced at the sight. More sceptical people thought it was tiny excrement that some idiot had once again shot into space.

'They all met their end. Their absolutely certain, simple end. And like all near-death experiences, this one also resulted in extreme changes. People, nations and organisations were given a second chance. A gift more precious than ever before.' He pauses briefly. 'And when they woke up again, they began to unwrap it.'

Yes, Christmas.

Which should have been their last. If it hadn't been for her: a person who had taken on the whole world and its hatred.

Latour still remembers the Ave Maria, which in some parts of Austria is only allowed to be played at Christmas because it is so precious. He sang along quietly.

A gentle smile appears on his face, followed by the urge to weep hopelessly.

If I had known back then that a young girl somewhere in Bavaria would save the world from destruction, I think I would have sung louder.

'The reactions to this event could not have been more different. People made decisions depending on their nation, cultural background and character.'

'Some carried on as before. But those were the fewest. The British, for example.'

'Others decided to turn back the clock. To see life as so precious, so worth protecting, that they took radical measures to preserve this world.' Latour knocks demonstratively against the wood of the glider and gives When an appreciative look. 'Many Buddhist countries were among them. Which seems strange, since they were the ones most likely to renounce this world. The Free State too, of course. Which is less strange.'

Sras smiles, as does When, but he can't quite hide his sorrow.

He certainly remembers the time of upheaval in Bavaria, the diplomat thinks. He knows how everything was on a knife-edge. Even with Melianne as the figurehead, even with the inventions and the new leaders, almost everything had nearly ended in disaster.

'But the rest,' he continues, 'decided for themselves that

nothing in the world makes sense, that it was all just a ride to hell. With the inevitable end.'

Yes, When thinks. They were given the greatest gift: a glimpse into the void, always reserved for the greatest saints. For good reason.

'So they decided to enjoy the ride. To do everything they could to sell themselves as dearly as possible on this earth.'

Latour looks demonstratively upwards. At the steel tubes that carry the greedy through the world. Slowly, this grey ceiling descends towards the ground.

The diplomat remains silent and leans back.

'I understand,' says When thoughtfully. And he really does understand. He has felt the fear of the people, his own fear at the time. Sees the cause and its effect.

No more time to lose. No responsibility. Only freedom, hedonism at all costs.

Frugality was for weaklings. He remembers the wars, the rebellions. Everything that had been postponed bursting out in a few days.

He looks outside. Somewhere back there lies his world. A world of silence, of peace, albeit with minor flaws.

And in front of him? What is waiting for me there, he thinks darkly. Am I supposed to bring peace to this chaos?

Suddenly he feels empty. And vulnerable. Too small for this task. Like this glider: a small fish among all the giant sharks.

I am not my sister. Even if everyone would like me to be. And I will never be able to replace her.

What can I do against a world full of passion and anger that has nothing to lose?

His heart constricts. Suddenly he feels a hand resting gently on his arm. When looks into Sras´ ice-blue eyes.

The pilot is silent, but When feels his overwhelming compassion. Even the diplomat smiles encouragingly at him.

'My humble self hasn't decided yet, which way to go, by the way,' he says with a grin, again with the nonchalance of a stockbroker. 'But I think I'll have to do soon.'

Greater Frankfurt

'Please fasten your seat belts,' says the pilot, his good humour back. As if someone had come up with the idea of unbuckling their seatbelt.

'I hope the mission has really been approved. We are now approaching Greater Frankfurt. I'd be surprised if our friends from the banking conglomerate wouldn`t at least politely enquire what we're doing in their airspace.'

Esteban (at some point during the flight someone was polite enough, it was probably Sras, to ask for his name) looks at the antiquated radio and then into the sky ahead of them.

A long string of landing planes can be seen, suggesting one of the still largest intact airports and cargo harbours somewhere around there. When doesn't know where to look first. Everything is so different. Fascinating or different? he wonders.

The ground is so grey and black, so little green and bright. Huge Autobahnen cover the earth like arteries, pumping the grey mass across the land, unless there is a traffic jam, which is the case pretty much everywhere. He can only imagine the noise down there, but he can feel the constant, restless vibrations deep in his heart.

Everything vibrates erratically and frantically. Hectic engines and thrusters, even the buildings seem to have been erected in a hurry.

And the people?

It's hard to see them behind all the metal, ponders When. He already longs for the daily sit-ins and giant satsangs of his homeland with thousands of people, who can probably even be seen from space.

And suddenly it appears on the horizon: the Frankfurt Skyline.

When has heard of it and thought it presumptuous to declare a few buildings a skyline. But now, even at a distance, there is something majestic about them that he cannot deny. But what does he know, the Alter Peter and the former BMW headquarters being the tallest buildings he has seen so far.

'A bit intimidating, aren't they?' says the pilot as he looks at When with amusement. 'They're even more impressive at night. Like old giants. Especially with their flashing blood-red eyes.'

'What's their purpose? Apart from being big.' When looks sceptically at the top of a skyscraper and thinks it does indeed look like a pencil.

'Before the overthrow, they were bank headquarters. Same to-day. Only now these banks are also the masters of the city. So this is a kind of government building now. I could fly closer, but there are probably already enough crosshairs on us. The thermals around this thing are also very modest.'

When smiles gratefully. 'No, thank you very much, brother. Just stay on course.'

Esteban nods and looks at his instruments again, while When leans back.

Frankfurt.

He wants to find out more. But Latour is sleeping, very peace-fully in When's opinion, and Sras at least seems to be asleep, even if he notices that she is doing some kind of breathing exercises - consciously or unconsciously.

So he activates his LB and sets it to visual mode.

The hologram of a small, cheeky boy appears and starts chattering away in a rush. 'How was Quasimodo? And how does it feel to have taken away a robot's greatest opportunity for heroism?'

His LB has taken on the appearance of Gavroche, another of Victor Hugo's heroes. How fitting, When thinks, and decides to listen to an audiobook by this Frenchman at home.

'Almost boring,' he appeases LB. 'And you're still too young to be a hero. And in the wrong country.' When smiles. Whoever came up with the idea of giving these technical grab bags a character really had a sense of humour.

'Well, since I'm here, by Rousseau, how can I be of service?'

'I'd like to find out more about the city of Frankfurt. And the greater Frankfurt area,' he says gratefully.

'We're not in the greater Frankfurt area by any chance?'

'By chance, yes. That's why I'm interested.'

'I see,' nods the little boy with the hat and takes a theatrical breath.

When has to laugh. Should the Council ever have to deal with the rights of artificial intelligence again, they would find an excellent defender in his LB.

'So: The city of Frankfurt first appears in the year 794 under Franken Furt. A Furt, you need to know, is a shallow crossing - in this case over the Main. And Franken meant the Frankish kingdom.'

'Thank you very much,' interrupts When, 'but I might deal with the older history later. I'm more interested in the period after the upheaval.'

And how the city survived while so many others were reduced to rubble, he thinks.

'I understand. Then I'll fast-forward a bit.' The boy wrinkles his nose. 'No time for depth, these brothers.' The hologram points to the outskirts of the city. 'I hope that changes again when we get back home.'

Yes, When thinks. I hope so, too.

'The official founding date of Greater Frankfurt is not exactly known.' Little Gavroche now has glasses on his nose and waves his arms like an 18th century philosophy professor. 'What is certain is that they were the ones who acted the fastest. As if the plan to seize power had been in place for a long time and they were just waiting to put it into action.'

'Like our Order', When muses a little guiltily.

But why should he feel guilty if the Order was only preparing for the inevitable and was ready when no one else was?

'Yes. But no more interruptions, please.' The hologram wrinkles its nose. All that's missing is him hitting When with a holographic stick.

'First, important nodes were brought under control. Captured would be a better term: the airport, the main railway station, the DE-CIX Internet hub. Virtually and in reality, the city disappeared from the scene for two days, after which everything changed.'

When wants to say something, but controls himself. Still better than a dry encyclopaedia entry, he thinks, as if there were any conscientious entries about that time.

'The executive forces must have been on call for weeks. Professional mercenaries, security firms, even parts of the police and the military co-operated, that is, they defected. And two days later, the mayor officially handed over the keys to the city to the new masters on behalf of the FRG. Frankfurt became a sovereign city again after centuries. There was not a single fatality, only a few injuries. A few houses were damaged by some nationalists, but nothing earth-shattering. There had been even more collateral damage when Eintracht Frankfurt was relegated to the second division once again in the past.'

'Football?' asks When.

He is familiar with the concept, albeit only vaguely.

'Exactly. I thought I'd embellish my presentation with a few examples,' says the Hologavroche vainly, suddenly holding a Bratwurst and an Ebbelwoi, a local cider, as he explains.

'Yes, very nice, thank you very much.'

He thinks about what exactly the LB said. Even in the Free State, there were more conflicts at the time of upheaval, When remembers.

'Does that mean the banks are the ones who did something good?'

The lecture seems to be over, and the KB apparently lets this further objection stand. 'Obviously. Apart from London, there was no other city in the world for which the upheaval was so harmless. Just think of Paris, Rome or Madrid. And since then, the banks seem to have everything under control. You can take that almost literally. No one can mess with them, certainly no one who wants to trade or move around. No one who wants to survive. The whole of Europe is far too dependent on them for that. Like us right now - by the way.'

When nods.

A faint beeping echoes through the cabin, but he pays it no further attention.

'And who has the power now?'

'Officially, a city council of six people, all former members of the big banks. Very powerful people, so there's a good chance they really do hold the power in their hands.'

The beeping gets louder and Esteban seems to get a little nervous.

'Ah. They're here.'

Without another word, When switches off the LB, already looking forward to the next lecture.

A wave of air pushes the glider downwards, but Esteban skilfully compensates for the turbulence. Sras is wide awake again
and imperceptibly nudges Latour. The diplomat wakes up.

When looks up and sees the shadow over their glider, which
looks like a giant falcon.

'Good morning and welcome to the airspace of the sovereign
city of Greater Frankfurt,' a woman's voice comes out of the
speaker.

Somehow she sounds nice, When thinks, like a kind usher at
an underground stop. However, an usher might have a little flag
with her, but not a fighter jet fully loaded with streamlined and
oval thingies hanging relaxed on its wings.

'Thank you very much for the warm welcome.' Latour is wide
awake, has grabbed the microphone and put on his most en-
gaging smile.

It's almost a shame, When thinks, that the fighter pilot probably can't see it.

'Our control center is having some trouble picking up your
transponder code.' When could swear there's a bit of mockery
in her voice.

'So we thought we'd stop by and ask for the number of your ...
flying object and your purpose of travel.'

When doesn't know who she means by we, but this time he's
absolutely sure there's a roar of laughter in the other cockpit.

'Of course. We're flight number AW4731 and we're on a hu-
manitarian mission for the Free State of Awaria. We are heading for the county of Hesse Nassau. Rendezvous with an aid
transport.'

'Thank you very much, AW4731. We'll check it out shortly.'
The radio cuts out, but not before When hears something in the
background that sounds like: 'And from there they'll continue

with the horse-drawn carriage (then the aforementioned laughter again).'

To their right, less than ten metres away, another steel monster appears. Additionally to the rockets, it has also bombs attached to its wings.

'F-16,' Latour whispers to him. 'From the old US inventory. Not quite up to date, but still good enough for any conventional conflict.'

When nods.

'And the pilots must be flying aces if they can fly that slowly.'

And not blow us out of the sky with their exhaust jets, he thinks, but prefers to conceal the obvious.

'Flight number AW4731. Check completed. You have green light.'

Esteban breathes a sigh of relief. Latour looks as unsurprised as if he had won a card game with cards that he himself had dealt from his sleeve.

'Thank you very much, Greater Frankfurt.'

'We wish you a good journey and good luck. Visit Frankfurt again when you're in the neighbourhood.'

'We will on the way back. I promise,' says the diplomat nonchalantly.

And When is surprised that he doesn't invite her for an Ebbelwoi and a Bratwurst at the Römer.

Hesse-Nassau

When wakes up as the glider´s nose bends downwards.

'We are here. We're about to land at Breitscheid2 airport,' says Esteban. Latour and he have been chatting animatedly in Spanish during the flight.

The sky has darkened in the meantime. They keep bumping through clouds and can see very little. But that doesn't seem to bother anyone, remarks When, least of all the pilot, who has been sharing one anecdote after another in a very unbrotherly manner, making the diplomat smile from time to time.

When briefly considers switching on the LB, but decides against it when they fly through the clouds and a runway becomes visible. For the most part, it consists of grass like in Munich.

'This is not a commercial airport,' Latour answers his questioning look. 'That's why your order could afford to land here,' he says with a smile.

Sometimes it is an advantage to be as insignificant as a blade of grass, the diplomat muses.

Apart from its eventful history, Latour remembers, the new county of Hesse-Nassau has little to offer. What was there passed relatively inconspicuously into the informal possession of its powerful neighbour - for its protection, of course.

The ground quickly approaches, and as they touch down, When almost feels a little nostalgic, so beautiful was the view from the glider down to the world below.

We must not stay out of the fate of mankind, he remembers the words of his instructors. We would like to, but the times when we lived as hermits in some cave or deep forests are over. We have to go out into the world and put our acquired skills to the test.

'Oh, my bones,' groans the diplomat. 'We're going back on a private jet. First class.' Stiffly and awkwardly, he wriggles out of the cabin.

Sras glides out of the cockpit like a snake, relaxed but with quite a potential for action.

59

Esteban carefully checks the cabin again to make sure nothing has been forgotten, while When sees a small group - perhaps a delegation, dressed as smartly as they are - approaching in a limousine with the top down.

An electric car, how thoughtful, he thinks, while everything else north of Quasimodo is burning more oil than ever before, as if burning fuel is a new national sport.

They gratefully say goodbye to Esteban from Colombia, with a sister in Bukaramanga; a mum who also owns a small restaurant there and is so proud of her boy that he made it from the German school there to the development academy in Munich, even if she doesn't understand what the people there are learning and, above all, what his new eating habits mean (she still tries to send him her homemade tamales, without meat, of course).

Latour in particular shakes his hand warmly, apparently Esteban's life story really made an impression, When thinks with a smile.

'I wish you a safe journey and much success in whatever you do. Unfortunately, me and the Neinhorn have to get back home and can't wait. Tomorrow my friend will be dismantled and sent back with me.' He smiles almost guiltily.

'No problem, brother. We'll find a way back,' Sras says gratefully.

'At worst, by train,' Latour replies with a smile.

'Thank you very much, brother.' When bows deeply. Go in peace.'

They both look at each other for a long time, as if it were the last time. One of the first lessons you learn in the Order, he remembers. It is always the last time.

'Are you coming, friend When?' Sras is already sitting in the brand-new car and is greeted warmly by a short, plump man.

Thin drops begin to fall from the sky as When takes a seat in the car and warmly greets the driver, who nods coolly, and another lady, who even has a bouquet of real flowers ready.

'Welcome to the County of Hesse Nassau. We are delighted to be hosting members of the Free State of Awaria - even if the pleasure will only be brief.'

Smiling, she sends an order to her LB and broadcasts the programme for this evening and the next day.

Banquet with the new count, a local business mogul who has bought the whole county out of love for his Lahn-Dill homeland, as Latour whispers to When in the meantime. Then a tour of the fortress in the historic centre of Dillenburg and a visit to a very important tower.

The diplomat takes a quick look at the list, then turns to When. 'It's a good thing I know my way around here myself,' he says conspiratorially. 'Tell me, brother, have you ever been to a proper pub?'

Dillenburg

The U-Boot, a fitting name, Latour thinks to himself, still in his smart dinner jacket, as he steps down three short but crucial steps (especially when you're not quite in control anymore, for whatever reason) into the small pub.

Sras follows in a short but very stretchy black dress for emergencies (whether inn brawl or ninja mission, always very useful) and holds the door open for When, the embodiment of modesty in his uniform. Simple, short stand-up collar, colour too orange for a uniform steeped in history (and Latour hopes the Order doesn't go THAT far to recycle usable clothes), but also too brown to evoke any thoughts of Tibetan traditions. It shows modesty, but also discipline, Latour thinks.

Discipline is also demanded of the poor brother as soon as he enters, as acrid tobacco smoke penetrates his eyes.

The boy smiles bravely, because he is a boy, as the diplomat has realised by now, and surveys the interior.

A rectangle opens up in front of them, about six metres to the left and right, but at most a comfortable two metres lie between the entrance and the bar, which reduces the time from entering to ordering to almost zero seconds, and also extremely shortens the way from one of the numerous occupied chairs to the fresh air waiting outside.

Most of the bar stool inhabitants have turned round and are scrutinising the intruders - especially laying eyes on the woman in the black dress. Latour almost has the feeling that one of these miniature hay bales is about to blow through the picture.

'Close the door. We don't heat here for the Frankfurt monkeys,' a mighty voice echoes from a storeroom. Shortly afterwards, a giant steps out, a barrel in each hand. 'Welcome,' they are greeted. The roof of the pub shouldn't have been a millimetre lower, because even as it is, the blonde mop of hair of the innkeeper (and it's probably the innkeeper, Latour guesses, otherwise it's more likely the promoted bouncer) is already touching the ceiling.

'Free choice of seats, ladies and gentlemen, this isn't the Hilton,' he says, a broad smile on his bearded face. 'How about right at the bar?' Invitingly, he points to three free stools right on the periphery of the taps.

'Thank you very much,' replies the diplomat, throwing his jacket over one of the stools, gallantly taking Sras' coat, which she has not worn all evening, then smiling encouragingly at When.

The rest of the guests have probably found them acceptable and turned away again, which may be because all sorts of strange people are passing through here, Latour reckons.

And because they follow the giant, which he would know even if he hadn't attended thirty-seven seminars in group dynamics.

Who can blame them, the diplomat smiles to himself as he orders three Altschuss and watches with fascination as the bartender´s paws skillfully pour the black liquid into the fragile and delicate-looking glasses.

'Your Altschuss. Cheers.'

Smiling, Latour scrutinises his companions as he passes on the foaming mixture of Altbier and coke.

When is looking at the walls, which are covered to the last centimetre with pub slogans, greeting cards and pictures from decades of pubs gone by, with amazement. Sras, on the other hand, has her usual opaque gaze with which she takes everything in. This time her attention seems to be focussed on the landlord. Latour involuntarily wonders how wide and tall the most challenging of her opponents was that she has ever sent to the mat.

Then her eyes wander through the bar, past the men still in their work uniforms standing in front of the small glasses of clear liquid, to a group in uniform, emblem unknown, perhaps a security company. Her eyes linger there briefly, before she notices Latour's gaze.

'It's nice here,' she says, beaming, and reaches for the glass. He nods at her with a smile.

Yes, it's a bit different from the elegant reception at the Dillenburger Kebab Palast, even if they have gone to great lengths with the vegetarian platter and vitamin-rich smoothies.

'It's an honour for us to welcome a delegation from Bavaria ... er Awaria,' the mayor had repeated, looking particularly at When.

And why not, Latour ponders as he looks at the somewhat overwhelmed young man.

How would I feel if I met the brother of a saintess? How did I feel? Did I even realise it?

'How do you like it here, brother?' asks Latour, bringing himself back from his thoughts.

How can he even like it here? he asks himself, almost a little guiltily. How can he block out what the world expects of him?

'Very interesting,' replies When, smiling and rising his glass. Then he gives the diplomat a brotherly pat on the shoulder, and Latour admonishes himself not to look so expressive in the presence of these strange people. Or to think so loudly.

'Appearances are a little deceptive,' says When with a smile. 'Many of us were disciplined pub-goers before the upheaval came and we finally saw the light. I'm no stranger to pubs either', even if he tended to sneak in there to relieve the befuddled pubtists of their cash, When recalls; and he thought it was a noble deed even then, as more money would have led to even more alcoholism. 'Some of us still talk about beer,' he continues, thinking of his revered teacher.

'And in our part of the academy, drunken boxing is even a course we have to take,' Sras interjects into the conversation, having charmingly declined an invitation from one of the uniformed men to dance - wherever the dance floor is supposed to be here in the pub.

'Seriously?' The diplomat orders another round, reassured that he will probably be the first to end up under the table.

'Yes. Only those students who have defeated three opponents at one per mille, two at two or one at three per mille pass the test.' She smiles mischievously at When, who smiles back conspiratorially. Then her smile disappears for a millisecond as she looks over her shoulder at Latour.

Apparently, the brave soldier has called for reinforcements and dares to launch another attack, the diplomat concludes razor-sharply. Less than two seconds later, two of them are already standing guard and Sras' gaze, although still lovely to look at, is no longer quite as charming as before.

'Maybe it's time to go,' remarks Latour and drains his beer glass in one go. 'You're just too beautiful for this evening, my dear.' He hands her the coat while When, who apparently hasn't had the same training as his sister, peers around the pub in a beery mood.

'Any problems?' the giant asks helpfully. One look from him and the troops, previously ready to attack, start to retreat.

'No, thank you very much,' says Sras politely, while the diplomat pays. 'But you really should have more women here,' she advises with a smile. 'That would certainly lighten the mood and take the burden off the few women who come in here.'

'Yes,' says the innkeeper, frowning. 'I don't understand that either. We're even having ladies' night tonight.'

'Tired?' the diplomat asks Sras after they have said goodbye to When.

Brave, this boy, decides Latour. The mood-killer LB and his chemistry have been dutifully discarded, and yet he hasn't wavered or put a foot wrong since we left the pub. He hasn't said much, but with him and his serene brothers and sisters that can mean anything from deep contemplation to pacifying hordes of testosterone-fuelled alpha males. At least that is Latour's hope, even if he is more than convinced of his own abilities.

'No,' replies Sras, trying to remember a time when her body still dictated her when it was bedtime, not the other way round.

'Then how about a historic tour in the moonlight?' He glances at the driver of their coach, who remains silent, which the diplomat takes as saying yes to a 24-hour service. The moon may not be shining, but he just finds the phrase so beautiful.

'Sounds interesting,' she replies and gets back into the car. 'The tour at lunchtime today was...' she searches for the right words.

65

'A little dry?' he comes to her rescue.

'Theoretically,' she replies, nodding imperceptibly.

'And you prefer the ...' He hesitates.

'The proactive part?' she completes this time. 'Yes,' she confirms, 'and especially when there's fighting.'

He smiles. 'Then I've got something for us. Driver, please take us to Wilhelmslinde.'

The carriage rolls slowly over the cobblestones. The smell of horses announces the famous Gestüt. Then it goes up the Schlossberg. No oncoming traffic, the lights are orange.

The Wilhelmsturm appears behind a few houses. Another pencil, Latour thinks, only not so high. And rather lonely and silent in the darkness.

'The tower is not our destination,' he says quickly, almost fearing a bored look from his companion.

'I know.' Sras smiles back.

How she knows, he has stopped wondering some time ago.

Then the car stops at a small road with a metre-deep gully, which the chauffeur has elegantly passed. The brakes let out a sigh as they engage. The driver nimbly opens the door for them, and only now does Latour notice the robust physique of their companion and the barely perceptible bulge in his jacket.

'Thank you very much,' says Sras, straightens up and looks at a, what shall we call it?, she ponders, and decides in favour of the term tree. Yes, definitely a tree, very old, emaciated, with a small rotten bench right under the trunk. Which is fine, because the branches, which really look like they are about to fall, are so thin that they really couldn't hurt anyone.

Smiling, Latour stands next to her, two pilsners in his hand.

If he has a secret power, she thinks as she smiles and grabs one of the bottles, it is to conjure up alcoholic drinks. She also noticed a black, inconspicuous bottle on the plane.

I hope, friend, you can do better than that.

'You can call it a day now,' he says somewhat patronisingly to their driver. 'We'll walk back.'

'Very kind of you,' he replies, gets behind the wheel and stays there.

Aha, thinks Latour, a chaperone.

He smiles, a little pained, and frantically pushes away the memories of those times when a chaperone looked over his and his companion's shoulders. And the times when it would have been better if someone had actually been paying attention.

'May I present: The Wilhelmslinde.'

She would try to look impressed if she knew how to do it. So she just smiles, which is usually enough, takes a sip and wonders about the bitter beer and an information board leaning inconspicuously against a flat wall.

A sudden movement next to her causes her neurones to fire from all ankles. But she controls herself as the diplomat runs to the parapet and shouts 'Better Türk than Pfaff' at the top of his voice.

Smiling apologetically and a little out of breath, he returns to her, and for a moment she feels disgusted by such lack of endurance.

Even the octogenarians in our country are better trained and can climb eight floors without panting, she thinks, and is again glad about the fitness check on lifts and escalators in her land.

'Excuse me. But this place always gets me.' He takes a swig from the bottle and invites her to sit on the bench next to him. 'I know the tree doesn't look like much, but this is exactly where a delegation from the Netherlands asked the infamous spider if he wanted to take up the fight against the Catholic superpower Spain.'

'The spider?'

'William of Orange. Even the anthem of the Netherlands is named after him.'

The Dutch War of Independence. She remembers the lessons.
Above all, the determination and brutality of the Geuse, who
even breached the dykes and flooded their own land to defeat
the enemy.

'How did he decide?' she asks, feeling gratitude welling up inside her. This really is a beautiful place, she has to admit.

'Of course he accepted. And drove the Spaniards out.' After a
long, hard fight, he adds in his thoughts. Needless to say, she
already knows.

'Honourable. His life here, the life he gave up to fight, must
have been comfortable, I take it?'

'I suppose so. But sometimes you have to give up safety and
comfort when freedom calls.'

She smiles at him with a mixture of gratitude and fighting spirit that makes him shudder.

Then she suddenly stands up, strides ladylike to the parapet
and shouts 'Better Türk than Pfaff' so loudly, that a dog starts
howling in some house down there.

Along the A45 motorway

The next morning.
Former motorway entry A 45, a number that has become mea-
ningless since the collapse.

Where the upheaval has kept the tarmac intact, local warlords
have set up their toll booths. A lack of maintenance has done
the rest to what was once Europe's showpiece motorway. So

the Autobahn maintenance department wasn't just there to put up cones to spoil the holidaymakers' mood at the start of the holidays, Latour thinks wearily.

But this part of the road seems to be in order and will at least take them as far as Siegen, as the mayor has assured them.

The diplomat rubs his eyes, wondering about his bad night's sleep last night.

Was it excitement? And if so, why? He was there in Yemen, accompanied the delegation to the Balkans, all worse than this situation.

'Good morning, mate.' Sras suddenly stands next to him and hands him a steaming brown drink.

She is no longer wearing a dress, rather a onepiece that looks more like a combat suit. Not the reassuring colours of the rest of the Order, no insignia. Just black and no frills.

He smiles gratefully, looks into her eyes, which shine as always, as if a source of inexhaustible energy is blazing behind them.

'Caffeine only belies the truth.'

He takes a sip. 'And what's that?'

'That you're tired and should have gone to bed earlier.'

He smiles like a schoolboy. 'I'll remember that.'

When, it seems to the diplomat, who definitely feels more at ease in drunken and equally drunk company he decides, seems to have coped perfectly with the last evening. He bids a grateful farewell to the delegation from the county, shakes hands and doesn't forget the least important servants, such as the driver, whom the diplomat can do without. He has decided he doesn't like him.

You have really embarrassing thoughts in the morning, he thinks. I hope they will never appear in your memoirs.

Then the Awarian stalks his troops like Napoleon - if Napoleon had had the aggressive charisma of Gandhi and his troops had consisted of three transporters fully loaded with power seeds made in Awaria and manned by five members of the Order. Among them is a boy who could be When's little brother and an older gentleman who Latour has the feeling he's about to have to help crossing the road. All five are unarmed.

For an order that has abandoned any notion of God, you have a lot of faith, he thinks to himself.

But apparently he is the only one who is a little worried about their journey to the underworld, because less than two minutes later, When comes towards him, beaming.

'Good morning, friend.' He bows deeply to the diplomat, then brother and sister smile at each other, beaming. Again.

'Good morning,' Latour smiles back and has the feeling that everyone else has heard an unspeakably funny joke this morning but him. 'Is everything ready?' He downs the rest of his coffee. Short-term solutions are also solutions, he thinks defiantly.

'Yes. The vans' batteries are fully charged. The cargo is securely stowed. Our sisters and brothers know the route and our destination.'

And hopefully everything that lies between us and there, the diplomat thinks anxiously.

'It's not going to be a jolly ride,' says Latour.

'No. But we know what we're up against.'

'Well then, what are we waiting for?' First he looks at When, then at Sras. He can slowly grasp the spirit. Must be the dark brew. 'I have to go to bed early tonight,' he mumbles.

Sras smiles mischievously at him.

When nods more seriously this time, then looks back at the

Wilhelmsturm, the Schlossberg with its ancient walls. He can feel the Dill rushing gently somewhere down there. 'I liked it here.'

Sras follows his gaze. 'Well, let's make sure you get back here safe and sound.'

Goodbye to the county of Hesse.

A sign on the side of the motorway with waving children and bullet holes. Apparently someone had too much ammunition left.

'Convoy Awaria. This is Hesse. That's it for us. Our authority ends here. From now on, you're on your own.'

'Understood, Hesse. Thank you for your help,' replies When into his LB, which is acting as a radio this time.

Latour, casually sitting in the passenger seat, looks in the mirror and sees the four jeeps heading for the exit.

Behind them, at the correct distance, the other vans drive, or rather creep slowly through the busy traffic, mostly overtaken by other lorries or the odd military vehicle.

He sighs as he looks at the speedometer. A solid sixty kilometres per hour.

By the time we reach our destination, the bomb will surely have rusted out and we can return home being at peace, he thinks mockingly.

He had got behind the wheel with the morning's coffee boost, but quickly realised, along with everyone else in the convoy, that the snail's pace is not for someone who occasionally drives a Ferrari. Then it was Sras' turn, more out of curiosity, he reckons, because the brothers and sisters started to feel queasy and then he did too as soon as she discovered the accelerator pedal. And the horn.

So they agreed on When, who performs the duties of driver

and convoy captain very conscientiously.

'What's our next stop?' he asks his LB.

'Siegen. Distance just under twenty-one kilometres,' he replies promptly.

'What's the purpose?'

'Military inspection. Last base of the former armed forces.'

So the Wild West begins up there, the diplomat, who has never been this far north, ponders. During their journey, he also sees why: more and more often, they have to dodge potholes or drive round unfinished roadworks. Some of the resting areas seem to have been looted, others have been converted into campsites. The cars first become smaller, then more and more battered, up to crash car level, robbed of their tyres or simply burnt out.

'Details, please. Keywords military control, border area Hesse and former NRW.' When thoughtfully activates his LB again. On the horizon, unfortunately closer than he would like, clouds of smoke are rising. Not the small, pale-coloured ones, but large, jet-black mushrooms.

'The armed forces under General Reil, especially the air force, set up a demarcation line shortly after the designation of the Free cities, which roughly resembles the former southern and eastern border of the former federal state of North Rhine-Westphalia. Over time, some border posts became permanent bases. Airports were added. The same thing happened in the north by the Danish troops, who placed the former Schleswig-Holstein under their protectorate.'

'And the Benelux countries are positioned in the west?'

'Exactly, under the leadership of France. Their contingent is the strongest. Mostly paratrooper regiments, flying squadrons. The foreign legion.'

'The aim of all this?'

As if he didn't know, Latour thinks. Free cities, counties, even sheikdoms and clan-controlled territories were springing up all over Europe at the time. Nowhere, however, had they found such fertile ground and established themselves as successfully as in NRW. While no stone was left unturned in Berlin, these cities seemed to thrive here under various tribal leaders.

'Initially, the aim was to capture the area and destroy this new political structure. When this endeavour proved impossible after a short time, the general staff of the new armed forces decided to seal it off hermetically. Naturally, they refuse to recognise the city-states, as they now call themselves.'

'With success?' Latour's eyes follow two Tiger combat helicopters, supported by a few small drones, circling menacingly over a range of hills.

'Define success.'

Latour sighs inwardly. Somehow he doesn't feel like defining today. Especially not success in the context of military operations - if there even is such a thing.

'Are there any parallels in history that could be compared?'

'Except in times of war, a temporary encirclement like in the Barbarossa campaign? Unlikely. The dimensions don't match, but perhaps sealing off the Gaza Strip and the West Bank by the IDF fits.'

Shocks make the transporter vibrate. The choppers seem to have found their target. They swoop down like hawks and cover it with rockets.

Sras wakes up, watches the horizon. When keeps the van on course, but seems to be whispering something. His gaze is sad.

Palestine, Latour thinks. And we all know how that turned out.

Siegen

The last real outpost of the armed forces and the last beacon of civilisation, as sceptics would say.

The city consists almost entirely of roads, on which military vehicles and vans move forward in long queues. Former football pitches have become refugee camps. A relatively high standard that has probably come with time, the diplomat estimates, as he strolls through the pedestrian zone along the Sieg, drinks a cocktail in the Extrablatt and wonders about the films being shown in the cinema.

The city has held up well, he thinks as he surveys the intact buildings that still house ordinary shops, with an increase, of course, in shops selling anything from camouflage coloured clothes to prepstuff, preparing mankind for the coming apocalypse. If there is a next one.

Apart from that, the only thing that stands out is that the city is conspicuously ... religious. Not a street, he notices, without one of the various places of worship, from a Hindu temple all in colour to the numerous synagogues, a modest Buddhist shrine - which his gang has probably already checked out - and a mosque.

He walks towards a multi-storey building that has a conspicuous number of aerials installed on the roof and used to be a shopping centre. In good times.

The first thing he does, however, is to stop by his Fist of Peace troupe, who, in order to avoid any inconvenience, happen to have taken up residence with their vans in the backyard of a vegetarian restaurant (aha, not so coincidental after all, he muses).

Fist of peace. Of course, he would never call them like that, but somehow he has been missing the passwords and code names for himself and the mission ever since he has met these strange people who sit quietly in the evenings and ... What do they actually do? Meditating?

Let them, he thinks as he keeps his distance and observes the scene. They've earned it.

The day was exhausting, even if there's no reason to complain. The military checkpoints were no problem, apparently the negotiators were thorough, which anyone who has ever had to face the omnipotence of military barriers will appreciate. Although the guards were anything but enthusiastic about having to allow aid shipments for the potential enemy to pass through, and who could blame them, they could find nothing to complain about. They even refrained from harassment, which really surprised Latour.

He looks at the brothers and sisters, who are sitting there as silent and motionless as statues, and notices the guards, who also seem to be experiencing some kind of peace.

You've found the peace we're all looking for, haven't you, he muses. Isn´t it your greatest good for export?

And the youngest member of this group is only seventeen years old, an age when the boys used to be level fifty-four fortnite fighters, dreaming of a Lambo or hanging out at the bus stop with their cuties.

But you're not invulnerable either, are you?

He had only realised it with When. Not with Sras, but apart from too little hand-to-hand combat, nothing can harm her dazzling mood.

The others - perhaps less experienced ones - sensed it too. And the boy. They were crestfallen when they saw the helicopters. Nobody said anything, even the radio remained silent, but he felt it: dismay. A lack of understanding. Something they haven´t experienced in their world, but will know in the coming days, the diplomat fears.

With one last look at When and Sras, he turns away, watching Sras winking at him. As if it wasn't already dark and he wasn´t in a black suit.

He smiles back bravely, heading towards the HQ of the armed forces while deciding two basic things.

First: clothes make the man. And clothes make situations. He will go to the nearest BW shop today and buy some camo.

Second, every time he thinks he feels something from now on, he'll have a drink.

The General

'Whisky?' he asks, pouring two glasses without waiting for an answer.

Latour is on the top floor of the former City-Galerie, which is now the headquarters of the former armed forces of the Bundeswehr. Reinforced walls, armoured glass, two guards in Kevlar in front of the entrance.

'Yes, I'd love to,' replies the diplomat politely, trying not to sound too greedy.

Both men take a deep sip, and Latour quickly realises that the cheap bottle is just a disguise for a fine spirit.

The general points to an empty ashtray, then to a small box. 'If you want to smoke, go ahead. I've kicked the habit, bad for your health.' He smiles and refills their glasses.

Latour smiles gratefully, but doesn't reach for the precious box. 'I also need to work on my stamina,' he says, while unobtrusively scrutinising his counterpart.

Tall and wiry, he looks rather too fit for his perhaps fifty years. The general has short, grey hair and the obligatory hints of scars on his neck.

The lieutenant general looks briefly at a screen on which coded columns of data appear and disappear in rapid succession, then he moves conspicuously uncomfortable chairs closer and sits down.

'So, Mr Latour,' he turns to his guest. 'Related?'

'Unfortunately not. But a big fan.'

'Just like me. It's because of the military training, it doesn't hurt anyone.' Now it's the soldier's turn to scrutinise his counterpart. 'Served?'

'As a medic,' says Latour almost apologetically. 'I've done a few courses in self-defence, weapons training. I was a UN observer in Africa for a short time.'

'I see,' says the general thoughtfully. 'The UN. Those were the days. Sad, inefficient, embarrassing times. But this idea...' He hesitates. 'A dream.'

And Latour is not sure whether it is pure sarcasm that resonates in the soldier's voice.

'So, pure philanthropy brings you here to our lovely neighbourhood? Your bosses must have gone all out. For permission, I mean.'

Latour thinks for a moment. Senses that a game has begun. Finally again.

'Yes. The Free State of Awaria is very keen to maintain friendly relations with all European powers.'

'Even with those who are not recognised and stand for hatred and terror?' the general asks. His voice is calm but firm.

'Are you asking me as a diplomat? Or as one of the representatives of the Free State?'

'Does that make a difference?'

'Yes,' says Latour with a smile, thinking back to the past few days. Did he even understand what was going on in this country, the former high-tech centre of Germany? And Europe?

Has he put up a fight? Or has he already given up, does he want to give up and submit to the calm that he has felt since the first day there?

Felt! Sighing, he takes a big gulp.

'As a representative, I would take the position of the Council of the Wise and say that it is precisely those lost communities that need to be led onto the right path. With help and not with the sword.' He remembers Adenauer's quote, which is written in dark letters at the entrance to the Centre for Diplomatic Relations.

'And as a diplomat?' asks the general, who has probably already exposed him as a mental sloth due to the many unnecessary pauses. 'After all, you have plenty of experience. In the field, too.'

Diplomat, Latour ponders seriously. Am I even still a diplomat?

'I would have to say that once the conflict has escalated to a certain degree, a helping hand is only seen as a weakness.' He hesitates. Appeasement. The Second World War. There are countless examples. 'And this is seen by the aggressive party as an invitation - for more violence.' The general is silent, then nods. 'We couldn't have put it any better.'

You could have, the diplomat thinks with a smile. And you did. And you acted accordingly, which is very rare.

'Hence the containment policy, as the Americans would put it?'

The general nods and calls an aide, who begins to project various images and statistics onto the walls.

Latour recognises maps with information on friendly and enemy troop bases. The enemy area is a triangle with Cologne and Dortmund as corners. A circle, almost as accurate as the legendary outer circle of a triangle used to tease children in maths lessons, shows the allies, or whatever they call themselves, protecting - or supposed to protect - the rest of the environment from the new alliance of cities.

'We screwed up. Or rather the Bundeswehr, when it was still

called that.' The general sets his glass aside gloomily, picks up a laser pointer and scans the line with the small red dot.

Latour almost has the feeling that the soldier is now with his troops, shaking hands with everyone.

'The upheaval came quickly, but we should have foreseen it. Weeks, months, even years beforehand.' He seems to remember. 'But by the time we received the order to advance, to wipe out the new powers before they could form their ugly roots, it was already too late.' The red dot approaches Dortmund, Düsseldorf, then Cologne. 'They were organised and well armed. And they had an influx of thousands of professional fighters from all over the world.' The general switches off the pointer.

Latour now understands why he is here. He smiles amiably and wonders whether it is sometimes lonely at the top, even - or perhaps especially - when you are surrounded by like-minded people.

'We lost at the gates of every big city. The losses were too high, so we retreated. We could have bombed everything to rubble, but my superiors decided against it.'

For a moment, the diplomat wonders whether the general approved of the decision at the time.

'We have held this line of defence that we took at that time ever since. We're trying to do what we can to limit the damage. To contain it, as you put it earlier. It's working, but nothing more.' He turns back to the diplomat and looks at him sharply. 'Which brings us to you and your welfare mission.'

'And the children suddenly realised how lonely the poor old woman had been all those years ago.'

Latour is back at the veggie camp, as he secretly calls it. The sisters and brothers have finished their meditation and have now arrived at a kind of communal get-together. Which seems strange to him, as he simply can't imagine a cosy evening without digital entertainment. Curious, he joins them in the circle. Even the sentries are sitting there, he notices, their weapons slung over their shoulders, now holding something made of tofu.

'Please go on.' He smiles at the storyteller, the older brother with grey hair and scholarly glasses.

Everyone smiles at him only Sras is missing.

'So they stopped fighting and started talking to the old lady.'

When sits down next to the diplomat and hands him a vegetable skewer.

'And they learnt about the suffering the old lady had been through in recent years. The woman told them about her children, who had left her to find happiness in the city and whom she never heard from again. Of her favourite deer, which lost her mother, and which she fed and cared for and named herself, watching her grow, only to lose her later to greedy hunters. Like so many of her animal friends. And again she was alone.'

The narrator pauses.

'This was also the time when she painted her house in a frenzy, as if everything was made of candy. We humans do strange things when we feel lonely.'

He looks around.

Agreement. Sympathy.

One of the guards has stopped eating. 'I should pop round to see my grandmother again,' he mutters. 'She's not the freshest and she lives in Offenbach. But she still makes a Sauerbraten tasty as hell.'

'Yes, you should,' the second guard interrupts him and points to the speaker, who continues slowly.

'The old lady never wanted to harm anyone. But she didn't want to be alone either. The children understood that and saw that all violence, all hatred is born only of fear. Out of fear of suffering.'

Silence. Somewhere in the city, bells are ringing. Soon after, a choir can be heard. Midnight service, the diplomat thinks.

'So they decided to help the old lady. They took her in their arms. Helped her to repair the house. They built a flat for themselves and feeding troughs for animals in need. Over time, an animal park was created where people and animals could get to know each other. At some point, their parents came to this park, and when they saw their children, who had now become young adults with shining eyes, they regretted everything, cried and hugged each other. And when the old lady died, after many years of companionship and happiness, everyone stood at her grave. The children, their parents, the people from her former village. And her animals.'

One of the guards looks down.

Latour feels a warmth in his heart that rises effortlessly without him having to push it.

'And as they all stood there, a small child, and only small children see such things, saw a shining figure standing behind a tree, a beautiful woman, with silver hair and a crown of leaves and acorns in it. And she smiled at the child, and the child waved back. Then the figure disappeared.'

The silence is even deeper now, interrupted only by the second guard, who mutters that the Grimm fairy tales have always been too brutal for him.

The narrator looks worriedly at the sentry, then at Latour.

I'm okay, old man, don't worry, Latour thinks, knowing that the man will understand.

'To this day, this forest is enchanted. The water there is clearer than anywhere else, the trees strong, the animals young and free. People who hike there and lie in the grass on the meadows find healing, draw fresh strength. And peace.'

Clever old chap, Latour thinks to himself as he looks round at the group, who can smile again, albeit with wet cheeks.

'And the oven has never been used to roast a piece of meat

again,' says When and stands up.

Then all the previously silent throats chime out as if rehearsed: 'Only grilled cheese!'

In enemy territory

Latour watches thoughtfully as the last barriers in the rear-view mirror become smaller until they are just a pale line.

The armed forces' sentries have waved them through, and one or two have even saluted. This reminded the diplomat more of a farewell, the last salute to soldiers going on their last mission. The Kevlar waistcoats, the buzzing of the surveillance drones, the snipers and the anti-tank barriers did nothing to change his uneasy feeling.

Almost like the death strip in Berlin back then, he remembers. The Wall, as many have trivialised it - as if a simple wall could have kept people from freedom back then and not the self-propelled guns and mines.

'We should put the windows on blackout,' he hears on the radio and Latour recognises the voice of yesterday's narrator.

It has now lost its softness, he realises, and has become colder.

Sras agrees, presses a switch and the windows go black.

'Well, it's going to be quite a surprise when the enemy only realises at the last moment how many heavily armed people are waiting for them in the driver's cabin,' says Latour jokingly.

When, in their midst, smiles politely, but seems to be communicating with his LB - or doesn't think it funny. Sras is not smiling. It's probably because she really doesn't think it's funny, he ponders, embarrassed.

But she wasn't smiling last night either. Which may have been due to the bruises and swelling on her face. And her limping.

'Sparring,' was her only answer to his question about her condition before she disappeared.

Great, our mysterious fighting master, our last trump card in case things get ugly, is getting knocked out by a couple of grunts, Latour thought at that moment. He immediately felt selfish and shabby.

She didn't turn up that evening, and her mood hadn't been any better when the vans left.

When When had sat down at the wheel as usual, her gaze met him with a strengh that almost telekinetically removed him from the driver's seat.

She has remained silent and sincere since that evening. And Latour realises that he misses her smile more than he should.

'So, what brings a diplomat with a meteoric career into the service of a peasant state? 'Latour remembers. The general has dropped his commanding tone, perhaps because of the whisky. 'Not the money, I guess.'

'No.' Latour smiled.

'Love, perhaps? Men have done dumber things for it.'

'Guilty,' the diplomat admitted. 'But not this time.' He was surprised of himself at how convinced he sounded. 'The challenge, I think. Besides, I've always had a soft spot for underdogs.'

The general smiled. 'Then that was the right choice. I don't even give this construct two more years before it gets swallowed up. Or implodes.'

The diplomat nodded. 'I suppose so. Isn't it strange how many enemies you make when all you want is peace?'

'Maybe,' replied the soldier. 'But of course I'm not into peace. And not a philosopher either.'

And I'm no hero, Latour thought. And the sides I've chosen so far? Underdogs perhaps, but always with a chance of victory.

Or at least survival.

'And this mission? Delivering aid to an area that is basically in a state of civil war? Thanks to Chinese investors, it would be safer to cross the African continent at the moment.'

Everything went well for the first few kilometres, Latour thinks, and secretly knocks on plastic instead of wood, which he doesn't really care about.

Nobody spoke. Sras only growled briefly as When cooled her swellings.

The traffic is getting less and less, the vehicles are becoming more and more MadMax style, mostly with lettering that clearly assigns them to one of the civil war parties - as the general would say.

Finally, the sign appears in front of them. All in black with white lettering in old German: Geyer's black bunch rules here.

Wonderful, thinks Latour. If it were to say, let all hope be lost, maybe even in Italian, the whole thing would have even more hellish class.

'So, what can we look forward to once we have left the borders of civilisation?' Latour had asked the general.

Both were in the exhilarated phase - which is usually shorter than memory would have you believe.

'Or is this a typical border phenomenon like the evil Thracians behind the borders of Athens or the evil South Americans behind the border with Mexico?'

The general smiled. 'In fact, we tend to understate things here. Otherwise we wouldn't be moving in with at least five armoured vehicles. If we have to.'

'Now I'm curious,' said the diplomat with a smile, meaning that he is worried.

He had suspected some trouble after the Free State's report, but it all sounded more like rumours than reality. Besides, a rogue state was their intended target, so what difference would a few inconveniences with the local population make?

'It starts with a highlight,' the general began, completely in his element. 'Geyer's black bunch, ever heard of them?'

'Yes,' recalled Latour. 'A fighting unit during the peasant wars under Florian Geyer. They did a lot of damage. Before they were routed.'

The general nodded approvingly. 'Exactly. And the 21st century version 2.0 has pitched its tents up there. Not ten clicks behind our lines. We estimate them at around a thousand men. They're constantly on the move, armed with everything from small arms to stolen tanks from former BW stocks. Their command structure is weak, more like a poorly organised mercenary force.'

'And what is their goal?'

'I would have said they love chaos. Violence. They themselves would portray it as tyrannicide in their tracts.' He took a breath. Apparently there are things that upset even a warhorse like him. 'They were one of the first to take up arms during the revolution. Tracked down and liquidated hundreds of millionaires. Even some billionaires were among their victims. They didn't steal anything, but the executions were brutal.'

The diplomat remembered the pictures and a chill ran down his spine. 'Well, I'm glad we're as good as penniless,' he tried to joke.

The windows are sealed, now the cameras take over: one in the front, one in the rear and one on each side. The 360-degree view is projected onto the driver's windscreen. Which is hopefully bulletproof.

It's dusk outside. There is less traffic, but the drivers are definitely more aggressive. It's not the first time they've been cut off and mobbed. Another vehicle speeds past them, heads hanging out of the windows, weapons of various calibres are held aloft.

'Break formation.'

Their transporter accelerates slowly while the other two fall back and keep their distance.

Yes, thinks Latour, maybe at least one of us will get through.

Then lights appear thirty metres above the trucks. Two headlights, no rotor noises, but that doesn't surprise him.

And even before he has automatically worked out a suitable negotiating strategy, a volley from some machine gun sweeps across the motorway, tearing up the asphalt not ten metres in front of them.

'What kind of cowardly moneybags are we dealing with here?' a loudspeaker echoes, distorted like a clown's voice.

The helicopter has now adapted to their speed, it has stretched its snout towards them and the first silhouettes are becoming visible. Camouflage uniforms and big guys who seem to be having a lot of fun behind a really huge machine gun on a mount.

These are not regular units, Latour muses. The pilot has it in him, maybe a former one, but the rest are irregulars. The worst kind in war zones.

'We'd like to ask the illustrious gentlemen for a little chat'.

Then laughter and a bottle that crashes against their windscreen.

Wonderful, Latour thinks, and remembers Treasure Island, his favourite book back then. And a bottle of rum.

Flight reflexes take hold of him, his heart pumps adrenalin

through his body.

They won't just let us through, he thinks. They'll tear everything apart and do who knows what to us.

When the Khmer Rouge took over, they shot anyone who wore glasses, because glasses stood for intellectuals, and intellectuals stood for the bad influence of the West.

He secretly congratulates himself on his new uniform, BW jumper, black cargo trousers, even combat boots.

What could we do now? He thinks feverishly, but he's not even driving.

We have to break out. Zigzag, ram the helicopter. Where's an exit? Or drop back, become a wrong-way driver. You can't follow all the vans at once, he thinks, hopeful for a moment.

Sweat appears on his forehead as he looks into the rear camera. And sees two armoured vehicles, packed with gunmen, coming closer and closer, jeering and firing wildly.

'Pull over. We have no other choice.' The old man is calmer than Latour would have thought. At least he sounds calmer.

Their transporter slows down. Another volley hits the road in front of them, one or two bullets smash through their bonnet. Apparently the gunman is getting more impatient - or more drunk.

Then they come to a standstill.

The front camera is out, maybe a ricochet. The rear ones show the rest of their convoy, also motionless, the side cameras pointed at the armoured jeeps.

'Very courteous, gentlemen,' it booms mockingly again, this time close to the ground. So the chopper seems to have landed.

'My staff will now begin the inspection. In your own interest, I ask you to raise your hands and not make any hasty movements.'

Laughter again, and Latour ponders whether it's their wish to find a reason for the shooting. Or whether they need one at all.

So that's it then, he thinks, as the outside mic picks up heavy footsteps. Army boots approach the car. Then the door of their cab is ripped open. Angry shouting erupts, then gunfire sifts through the cabins. All the cabs.

And in a small wood somewhere further west, the old man has seen enough and switches off the cameras.

Sturdy oaks line the clearing, their leaves the colour of autumn. The moon is overcast, light shines only faintly from the three screens, which are powered down by the two brothers and one sister now that the horror show is over. They dismantle the joysticks as if they had done nothing else in their lives.

The diplomat breathes a sigh of relief and looks around. Apparently he is the only one who was upset. His comrades go about their work in silence, preparing their new transports for take-off. The three box-like or rather egg-like objects are three by two metres long, with wheels to make them look at least a little bit like a car.

Sras, who has finally been persuaded to wear appropriate bandages, looks bored. When discusses something with his younger brother, who has just steered a ten-tonne truck with a joystick as if he were Super Mario dodging barrels in Donkey Kong. Then his friend seems to notice Latour's gaze and comes over to him.

'You could have warned me,' says the diplomat, thinking about the sudden commands of the elder brother of the Order, who can apparently switch from fairy-tale uncle to super spy in

1.2 seconds.

He couldn't hide his surprise when the battle eggs rolled out of the backs of their caravans, each loaded with only two bags of super seeds (the rest was camouflage), apparently being more potent than meets the eye.

'We weren't sure we even needed this feint.' When smiles guiltily.

'Apparently we did,' the diplomat replies flippantly, even though he really can't be angry. After all, the trick saved their arse. He probably wouldn't have done it any differently and wouldn't have let an outsider in on it. 'And what's next? Do we unfold our folding bikes, which are hidden in the back of these ... things, in case someone tries to get at us next time?'

When laughs. 'I don't think so. But tricks and deception aren't my speciality,' replies When, looking towards the old man.

'Then we'll have to come up with something else next time. If we want to get there at all. This time was very close.'

Both are silent for a moment, and the diplomat wonders if he is the only one who finds it strange how precisely the robbers were expecting their convoy.

'Yes,' replies When. 'But it's not that far now. From Königsforst onwards, we'll be under the protection of the city council. Until then, we'll use the night and avoid the major roads. Our cars are four-wheeled, so we can get through anywhere.'

Latour has to smile when he hears his brother talking about machines, and even better, cars, for the first time.

So you also collected toy cars as a little boy and stood in amazement at a building site to watch the loud things with the big shovels.

'That sounds like a plan.' He nods at When, as hopefully as he can.

Then suddenly the older man stands next to him with his glasses, which he apparently didn't need for the remote control of the truck, and asks them to set off.

Just another nice storyteller, Latour thinks, shaking his head. Well, it can hardly be a disadvantage that their storyteller once lived in Pullach for a while.

Country roads.

Somewhere parallel to the A4 motorway, somewhere near the once picturesque little town of Reichshof.

'Is that all? Sounds like a walk in the park.' If you like walking through a minefield, Latour thinks grimly as the illustrious description of the balance of power that prevails in the Blue Banana comes to mind. The general has not promised too much.

Beyond the windscreen of their battleegg, which feels as uncomfortable as it looks, he can't see in the inky black night a thing; Sras and the others are driving with light amplifiers.

When has his eyes closed, so the diplomat also leans back and remembers.

'Not quite. Our contacts keep us constantly informed, so the information should be reliable.' The general had poured Latour another drink. In the meantime, the adjutant had brought a second bottle. 'Let's start with the upper part of the spectrum. I must have scared you off a bit with these black bunch bastards.'

An observation.

'A little. Yes.'

'But it didn't all go down the drain like that. Just most of it. After the Reichstag fire and the ultra-decentralisation, it was like a pistol duel between two trigger-happy cowboys. Whoever pulled the trigger first won.'

'Like in most places in the world. But for something like this to happen in Germany ...', said Latour, remembering the arrogant left part of his home country. The Algerian flag on the Eiffel Tower.

Nowhere else in Europe had the riots been worse, the police more powerless. Even the Legion could not have been everywhere. So the brave citizens took their fate into their own hands, as they had done for centuries.

'We had been sitting on a powder keg for decades. Who would have thought it?' says the general sarcastically. 'It all just happened so quickly. That's how it must have felt for the people after the shelling of Danzig. After the news that they were firing back.'

The soldier was silent for a moment.

Perhaps he wondered why we find it so difficult to remember times of peace when the wars tug at our thoughts so much.

'But back to the time after the fire. Many authorities stopped working in the first few hours. The homeland security regiments turned out to be inefficient. As expected, the police were overwhelmed. Interestingly, the fire brigade was able to provide a little calm.'

The general twirled the glass in his hand, letting the whisky slosh back and forth.

'Homeland Security was only able to hold Münster, their base, and a few neighbouring villages. Bonn was defended, mainly by resident Nato and UN troops. Most of them have left by now, but the city government there is relatively stable. The borders with Cologne are, of course, heavily guarded.'

Latour nodded. 'What about the airport? The Duisburg inland harbour? Eifeltor?'

'The airport is under Cologne's control. That's why you're travelling into the blue. If we didn´t restrict air traffic, the countless lunatics who are still taking everything out of the sky that appears on the horizon would do so. The harbour and the train station are under the protection of a business consortium: EON, Aldi, Bayer. There are always battles, but over the years it has really dawned on everyone that if you really destroy everything, there's nothing left to eat.'

He paused for a moment, sipping his whisky.

'That was the top end of the spectrum. In the middle, we have a lot of communities that had integrity and were unimportant enough to maintain the structures and therefore the peace. Brave mayors kept order. In others, the police had enough presence to establish themselves.'

Amtsknechtswahn is one of them, he muses, the name always bringing a smile on his face.

'Some major cities are under clan control. Or in the power of several clans. Or guilds. Or gaffs. But you already know that. Your group is going straight into their heart.'

The diplomat nodded a little sheepishly, no longer knowing whether to feel like a hero or an idiot. What the hell, he thinks. There's probably very little difference anyway.

Lower spectrum

'It gets really interesting at the bottom.' The general was now really enjoying himself. As if he were describing all the attractions at a theme park. 'It's like during a pandemic: from human to animal in forty-eight hours.'

The diplomat knew what he meant. The first was far from the worst, and nothing against the time of upheaval, but the first time is always special.

'Yes. People do strange things when they panic.'

In the beginning, it was just absurd. The hoarding, the empty shelves. But then the country leaders came and played dictators for a short time. Human rights disappeared as if they had never existed. Neighbours villainized each other, as in the best days of the GDR. Police officers became soulless followers of orders, beating old people through the alleyways and hunting down young people who were still on the streets at five past nine.

'And when order breaks down, everything gets worse. Much worse.' The general called in his aide again. Apparently even his memory couldn't cope with all the excesses.

'Wherever state power collapsed and the integrity of the community was not strong enough, tribal-like organisation usually took over,' the adjutant began his lecture. 'In the larger cities, these were the clans, which already had an excellent organisation to rely on. Hence their speed of action.'

The general nodded favourably.

'Corporations were able to defend their territory in various places and expanded using security and mercenary armies. Mostly in alliances. But the more rural and isolated the community, the more bizarre it became. Religious organisations often took over the official business. Churches and mosques became headquarters. This was often without bloodshed. Sometimes, however, sects were formed among the fanatics or end-time theorists. A cult with several hundred members has returned to Norse mythology and lives in the Teutoburg Forest like our ancestors. Eco-fascists have turned their organic farms into fortresses and hunt down anyone who isn't a flawless vegan.'

Latour smiled until he realised he was the only one. 'You're not joking?' he asked in amazement.

'No. And it gets even better.'

In comparison, my Afghanistan mission was really manageable, the diplomat thought back. There were only five different warring parties.

'In some castles, old noble families have proclaimed their rule again. With regalia. Audiences. The whole programme.'

'Interesting,' said Latour, because he didn't know what else to say. And because he wanted to banish thoughts of a descendant of Charlemagne who would suddenly stand before him on horseback, lance in hand, to proclaim the new Franconian Empire.

Peace 1

'One last thing.' The general spoke a few commands into his commlink. 'I'm a frontline soldier, but I'm not blind. I know that your mission and the simultaneous appearance of a nuclear bomb can't be a coincidence, no matter what my superiors try to sell me.' He paused and looked sharply at the diplomat. 'Especially not because I know who's accompanying you.'
 He pulled his handgun out of its holster and checked it. 'Patrol,' he said in response to Latour's questioning look. 'As I said, I'm a frontline soldier. So?'
 'I'm sworn to secrecy,' Latour replied seriously. 'But I don't like to hide anything from the only allies we have up here.'
 Concealment only really begins, he reflected, when the negotiations start. He weighs his words carefully.
 'So yes, it could be that the aid transport isn't the only mission we have. And I'm not the only one who can prove myself in the upcoming chess match.'
 The general nodded gratefully. 'Then it's him. Her brother.'
 Latour's face remained still, but the general's seemed to relax for the first time. Suddenly he looked like an old man.
 'Then I'm glad we were able to help.' He hesitated. 'I dreamt that night too. Like all of us. And my family too: my wife, my three children. She saved us all.'
 'Yes.'
 Both were silent, looking down.

A patrol took up position outside the room, waiting for their superior.

'I'm tired, my friend. So tired. I want peace.'

'Yes,' Latour replied quietly. Peace.

'It's more than just this bomb, isn't it? It's about all bombs. All weapons. And the fingers that will push the buttons. Or won´t.'

Once again, the diplomat didn't know what to say.

The general briefly shook Latour's hand. 'I wish you all the luck in the world. And him', he said and walked out of the door.

Then, back to now, Latour opens his eyes again wearily and sees the fire in the distance.

Abbendroth

'Get out.' Her voice is made of ice, her eyes are fixed on the mob.

Disorientated, but mechanically, the diplomat opens the door.

'I could ...' begins When.

'Too late. Too many.'

Now Latour hears the wild screams not two hundred metres away. Shadows dance around a fire, perhaps fifty or even a hundred.

'Pat. Kat. To my side. Lights out.' Sras takes off the night-vision goggles, then switches on the headlights, high beam.

'Roger that,' echoes from the loudspeaker, almost like digital voices.

Latour is outside. Gunshots ring out somewhere. He tries to rub his eyes, to wake up from this nightmare.

When also gets out now, the first time Latour has seen him in a hurry.

'Good luck, sister,' the boy says, fighting to stay calm. He reaches into his waistcoat and places a taser on the passenger seat.
 Sras nods. Her eyes are almost white. Then she presses the accelerator.

To the right and left of Sras, her sisters and their vehicles turn away, disappearing into the darkness for a brief moment.
 Sras strips off her shoulder bandage, takes a quick look at the taser.
 Another hundred metres. And the fire gets higher and higher, the screams of the figure at the top of the pyre louder.
 Too slow, she thinks as she tries not to waste a metre, to stay on the optimal line between herself and the witch.

When and the diplomat watch silently. The rest of their comrades are with them now.
 'They'll make it,' the old man says to him.
 Latour looks around desperately. A weapon. Just a damn gun. Then the barrage begins.
 Please, please be armoured, he thinks, not wanting to remember the weight of the battleeggs. And how easily they rolled down the ramp when they were unloaded.

Sras dives under the dashboard. The first shots are far away from target. Surprise effect. The next volleys whiz just over her, then smash into the windscreen.
 Good, thinks Sras. Already so close that they can barely miss.
 Then comes the first impact: human, human, human with a

gun, human again. Now she feels a pinch in her calf, then one in her shoulder. Then another heavy impact.

It must be the pile of wood, she realises as she is pressed into the harness and her breath stops for a moment.

Then she enters a world where thoughts are too slow to be valuable.

Even the lunatics this precious scene has brought together start to scream when the flimsy car drives into the crowd, rolling bodies over or hurling them away, crashing into the left side of the woodpile. The car is riddled with more than small arms fire, oil bleeding from its wounds. Grimaces, having overcome their shock, rush at the car.

Please, be alive. Please, get out, Latour thinks. No, please don't get out. Fly away.

He has tears in his eyes. He sees the burning pile of wood tilt and collapse over the car.

Then the door opens.

It literally explodes towards the first two attackers, who are catapulted backwards, still shooting wildly. A shadow appears, close to the ground, and five attackers fall as if the earth had opened up beneath them. Then the pack closes around her and nothing is visible for a moment.

Small flashes of light twitch in a duet while Sras, still in puma stance, ploughs through the crowd with tasers.

She sees the victim out of the corner of her eye. The pole the girl is tied to is now lying lengthways on the car, the fire licking at her feet.

Growling, Sras knocks out two attackers, uses the next one as a springboard and lands on the roof.

Always look for the high ground, a doctrine of warfare.

But not when you're surrounded by trigger-happy maniacs, she thinks, forgiving and cursing herself at the same time for the thought that may be her last.

Then the screaming begins anew, bodies fly through the air, are being run over, right and left.

Pat. Kat. Sras takes the opportunity to free the sobbing girl from her restraints.

More screaming. No more mad cheering, just screams of pain.

Good. Just what I wanted to hear.

Königsforst

The foothills of the forest slowly come into view. The sun is already rising behind them, penetrating the fog.

Latour is at the steering wheel, frantically trying to drive slowly. Next to him sits sister Jude. And Sras. Who has stopped bleeding all over the seats.

He tears his gaze away from her. He looks to his right at the second car, which is about as battered as theirs. In it sits the old man at the wheel, next to him the silent Kwint and the rescued girl.

And on the roofs, When and the rest of the group are holding on as bravely as they can, but Latour can literally feel the cold on their skin.

So he had tried to keep up a steady pace, all night long, even though his instincts tell him to put the pedal to the metal to get them to the hospital.

'We won't leave anyone behind. Never,' the old man replied to the suggestion of the two warriors, who seemed to regard each other as nothing but ballast.

'Think, brother,' Pat replied as she wrapped a bandage around the flesh wound on her arm. 'We've only got two vehicles left, and they're barely fit for the road. And Sras and the girl need a hospital.'

And you don't? thought the diplomat as he looked at the bruises on the little Irish girl's face.

'What do you say, brother?' she turned to When. 'Getting you to your destination is our mission. Everything else is secondary.'

Everything else? Latour suddenly thought sadly. Or everyone else?

'We're not leaving anyone behind,' When said firmly. 'Those of us who still have strength will go to the rooftops and make themselves secure somehow.' He looked at Latour, then at the old man. His voice changed, became cooler. 'You drive. Nice and careful.' Then he climbed onto the roof of one of the dented battleeggs. 'If anyone falls off, we'll let you know,' he said to Latour, forcing himself to smile.

So they had put a few kilometres between themselves and the mob. After the vehicle attack, the lunatics didn't look particularly combative, but better on the safe side. Besides, none of them knew what else would crawl out of its holes during the night.

After that they had finally rested briefly behind an abandoned barn.

Sras was already unconscious by then, the healer kneeling over her, apparently a combat surgeon from the front lines from the way she was wielding her scalpel.

'She's not unconscious,' Jude explained when she noticed Latour's worried look. 'She's just got her metabolism down to a minimum.'

And it was true. Her pulse was palpable, clear, but only at twenty beats, her breathing barely there.

Latour nodded gratefully at the medic and pretended to be reassured. 'What about the girl?' he asked, seeing her wrapped in blankets, staring into space while the boy checked her emergency infusion.

'Kwint's looking after her. She's in shock and dehydrated. A few burns, but she'll survive.'

Latour nodded. Pacing around the cars, checking tyres, engine.

'Will our rides hold out as well?' asked When.

'Hardly,' Latour replied, wishing he'd spent more time in garages when he was young. 'The tyre sealant spray worked. The oil leak isn't completely sealed, but it will do. You won't get much more for the cars, though, I'm afraid.' He smiled and hoped that the adrenaline would continue to flow through his veins until dawn. And that his brain wouldn't start working on certain things right now. If it was up to him, it should never start.

'We're ready,' said the old man. His glasses seemed to have gone missing. 'Let's hope we get a nice reception. And the nearest hospital isn't too far away.'

They quickly find the former railway line. Without any low-hanging branches, as Latour so gratefully realises. He has often looked up and into the rear-view mirror, but has only seen brave smiles and how they have held on to each other; the Irishwo-man, small but a body like a linebacker, who has held When rather than the other way round. Kat, the Russian, has her foot wedged in the half-open window, silently watching the vicinity.

But it's too early for unpleasant encounters. And there is too much fog. So they get through unmolested and without being checked.

Old overgrown bunkers appear out of nowhere, memorial stones can be seen, former hiking trail signposts rot in the dew.

Then Sras opens her eyes. The medic smiles at her, checks the bandages. Latour looks half at the road, half into her eyes.

'Did I miss something?' she asks a little weakly and straigh-tens up.

The meeting

'Send an SOS signal, Original ID,' the diplomat instructs his LB. If we don't find them, hopefully they'll find us.'

The forest has thickened, but at least the fog has lifted. A nice area for hiking, Latour muses, if the conditions were a little dif-ferent... that is, if the hikers were less wounded and tired than they are right now.

He tries to avoid potholes and bends around thick roots, but is only moderately successful.

'I'm all right,' Sras says, a little annoyed, as he gives her an-other quick glance. 'If you don't crash into the nearest tree, I'll be delighted.'

'I'll do my best,' Latour replies, more defiantly than planned. But if we've come this far...so let it be. 'That was the bravest thing I've ever seen.'

'It was necessary,' she replies, and the diplomat realises that

101

he will be terribly defeated when it comes to harshness. 'Besides, the chances of success were over fifty per cent.'

Only the chances of getting out of the pandemonium without any losses were not quite as high, he thinks.

'I would have liked to help.' He means it sincerely.

She laughs and holds her stomach.

The nurse between them, lifesaver a moment ago, is apparently trying to assume a liquid state in order to flow into the crack between the seats.

'Excuse me. That's really very kind of you. I haven't seen a chevalier like you for a long time. So honourable.' She calmed down again.

'And so stupid. I see,' he remarks dryly. Then he attacks. 'As stupid as letting yourself get beaten up just to look weak?'

She doesn't look surprised. 'That wasn't stupid. That was preparation.'

'For what on earth?'

'For our mission. How do you think, friend, will we get access to the negotiations. By asking?' She straightens up, looks at him sharply.

'I don't know. We'll think of something.' He tries to sound nonchalant.

'That's stupid. I had a plan. Some of the council members are martial arts fans and most of them are gamblers. I wanted to challenge someone. If we had won, they would have given us access.'

'And if we had lost?'

'I have no idea. I haven't thought about that.'

'Delegation Free State of Awaria,' suddenly booms from his commlink. 'This is the delegation from the Free City of Cologne. You're a bit off course, but as you like to say down there?

Das passt.'

Apparently everyone becomes a comedian as soon as they sit in front of a radio.

'Copy that, Free City of Cologne.'

'We'll send you the coordinates. You can hardly miss us. A medical team is standing by.'

'Thank you very much,' replies Latour, then he studies the incoming coordinates. 'Three kilometres to go,' he says and raises his thumb, but the other car must have been listening as well. Everyone beams at him. Even the doctor is smiling.

Only Sras scowls. 'If they think I'm going to lie down on one of their butchers' stretchers, they've got it all wrong.'

'I'll stay with you, sister. And with the girl.'

Sras nods gratefully.

'Well, at least you really do make an extremely weak impression now,' risks the diplomat, who somehow doesn't care about any social conventions right now.

They finally reach a clearing. Not a second too soon. By now Pat must be doing everything she can to hold the peacefully sleeping When, and seems to be in a trance, looking pale as a greek marble. The battleeggs` energy gauge is at two per cent and that's all the members of their group have left in their tanks either.

'Please stop, my honourable guests,' a man with a megaphone shouts.

Latour stops and sees the man with the device, tall and broad. Four men stand around him, rapid-fire weapons in their hands. Two paramedics in white are waiting behind the group. There must be more gunmen behind the trees, if he judges Sras's sharp gaze into the forest correctly.

No cars. Just a streetcar that looks like a battering ram from the Middle Ages, namend number nine.

Cologne

"I understand that you had to overcome certain ... difficulties on your way to our wonderful city?"

Latour almost has to laugh out loud. But that would echo too much in this reception hall that the representative of the representative of the representative of the deputy city council has chosen to welcome them.

Besides, his troops are now too formally dressed, washed, shaved and bandaged - stitched and taped, to be precise - for street manners to be an option now.

"Just a few," replies Joseph, the older gentleman, now apparently in his role as diplomat.

I have to say something quickly, Latour thinks with a smile, otherwise I'll be replaced.

"But that was to be expected," he interjects, extending his hand to his counterpart. It's about time I earn my money. "It's all the nicer to be here now."

The deputy smiles gratefully. "In the foreseeable future, our opponents will hopefully realize that our city and the League of Cities pose no threat, and air traffic will flourish again."

"We hope so too."

"If kerosene is still available," says one of the magistrate's companions.

Latour smiles dutifully.

"And your accommodation is to your satisfaction? Forgive the presence of the guards, but you have chosen a somewhat ... difficult time for your arrival. Today is the day before 11.11. And no matter how much this city is besieged, pillaged, attacked and humiliated, one thing will always remain: the carnival."

"We understand that very well. And the accommodation exceeds our expectations," says When.

Which may be true for someone who is comfortable in a tiny cell, the diplomat thinks, but nods in agreement.

"Your journey on the streetcar was pleasant, I hope?", their host asks again in a polite tone that has probably been rehearsed a thousand times in front of the mirror.

"Yes," confirms Latour before When can say anything.

Let me handle this, kid, you'll get to show your superpowers soon enough.

"Your city is very interesting."

Latour remembers riding in the battering ram while his eyes were half on his comrades, half looking through the armored windows of line nine. The damage from the terrible time of upheaval was still visible in piles of rubble and shattered house walls.

"And so refreshingly diverse."

Careful, Eric, no lies, don't lay it on too thick. Put the truth in a good light.

Which is difficult for him. The spaces between the individual dominions were too guarded. Most of the people were too slim, almost wiry. Except for the magistrate, of course.

"I'm very pleased that you like our city. The last few years have been difficult," a word that this guy seems to love, "but we people of Cologne are tough."

And he seems to be right. The diplomat has seen people laughing everywhere. Not the deep, attentive smiles like in Awaria, no, rather a cheerful, defiant smile.

Where was the last time I saw that? asks Latour, remembering.

And finally he admits to himself that he is thinking of her.

How she is probably taking a deep breath now so as not to complain about the clothes without stretch. He imagines her pacing up and down the room like a cougar who can hardly wait to beat up the whole of Cologne to get the bomb - or make peace, which probably plays a minor role for her, Latour reckons, but what does he know.

"Please forgive my loquacity, dear friends," says the deputy, who has probably not missed Latour's absent look. "You are still exhausted. Please get some rest. Tonight there will be a small banquet in your honor. Our escort will pick you up at 7 pm. We want you to feel as comfortable as possible before you start the arduous journey home tomorrow."

When, Joseph and Latour say thank you, leave the reception hall and get into the cars.

You're wrong, my friend, Latour thinks and feels a certain ... fighting spirit inside him. He also notices it in the old man's hawk eyes, and When's aura, which is ... kind of red, he thinks.

It will certainly be arduous. And we're going home again.

Just not tomorrow.

Hotel l'amour

There is indeed a large neon heart hanging above the entrance, and a romantic one it is, as it lacks all the arteries, valves and veins that make a heart so realistic and useful. And so vulnerable.

Unfortunately, it isn´t shining, When thinks. Ever since they entered the city, he has wondered about all the lights that are so superfluous when you learn to see in the dark. And realise how precious electricity is.

But this heart should glow, he thinks. Just like the statue of his sister in front of the Entschweren Academy or the hand in front of the Sisters' Unravelling Academy.

Do I miss home already? he asks himself as he watches their

escort drive away.

He looks through the streets, which are now in twilight, and feels the energies. But not the calm currents that run through Awaria, but rather suffering and pain and a defiant will that rises more and more, wants to spread and let off steam. Apparently the carnival is a really big deal here, he muses. As if we don't already wear enough masks and disguises in our ordinary lives.

'Are you coming, friend?' asks Latour, already on the steps of the small hotel.

'Yes,' says When, smiling, as he passes the dark heart.

Boy, the diplomat thinks to himself as he walks through the lobby and past the reception desk. With When at his side, he takes the first flight of stairs. Hopefully, the boy is starting to warm up.

They pass three floors of an apparently smoker-friendly hotel, as yellow as the walls are. They don't see any other hotel guests; tourism seems to have slowed down considerably since the upheaval. Except for disaster and war tourism, of course, which Germany would probably have traditionally liked to leave to other countries.

Kat and Pat stand in front of the door to their room - they have three, each with a double bed, but the girls seem to have made their room their headquarters - smiling as the best-looking doormen he has ever seen, the diplomat thinks. Perhaps he should give his father a hint or two when it comes to personnel decisions.

'Password?' asks the Russian woman with a look that would have silenced even an angry crowd outside a nightclub.

'Seriously?' asks the diplomat, confused.

Patricia looks innocently at the floor, When suddenly finds

some ceiling lamp incredibly interesting. And there it is again: the hawkish smile.

Kat winks at him. 'Right. You can pass,' she says and opens the door.

'Very kind,' replies the diplomat and smiles awkwardly back.

Sure, we're laughing our heads off at the outsider, he thinks. Because he never knows when we're playing the saints and when we're playing the comedians.

Then he enters the room, so inconspicuous from the outside. When is behind him, then Pat and Katja, who closes the door behind them.

Council of war

'Listening devices?' asks Joseph, the name apparently spelt with a ph and probably some kind of code name.

The boy, Kwint is his name, or that's what he calls himself, says no. In front of him are some devices that must have something to do with surveillance. However, Latour can't tell whether it's a device or part of a device.

The spy, or former spy, Latour thinks, looks questioningly at the window where Sras occasionally peers through a slit in the shutter. She shakes her head. No more bandages on her anymore. You wouldn't think that their journey had involved so many complications.

But you live in the present, I've realised that by now. The past is just a story that is being told. And you have to finish it. Preferably now.

'The girl is fine. She's being well looked after,' says Jude. She used to work inside the LMU after patching up soldiers on the battlefield in various conflicts. 'Her wish is to come with us.

To Awaria. I think that's a good idea.'

When nods. 'Yes. She's one of us, I sensed that the first time I saw her.'

'She won't be one of us, but sometimes you guys are useful for something,' says Pat, smiling at When.

He smiles back.

All right, so they slash out at each other too, the diplomat thinks contentedly, wondering when he last encountered polite and peacemaking bullies.

'Then we can begin.'

They form a circle again, as they did in Siegen ages ago. Only this time there are no stories being told.

'We've received information from our contact,' Joseph begins, and Latour wonders when exactly that might have happened.

Back in the day, when the US wasn't hidden under a blanket of billowing, corrosive fog that nobody knew where it came from, they found a nice word for an operation like this: Clandestine.

'As expected, the conference is taking place a day earlier than planned. All the participants seem to have already arrived in Cologne and are waiting. Except for one party, but we don't know anything about them anyway. Only that it is eagerly awaited.'

You're not as good a black ops uncle as you are a storyteller, but still, Latour thinks.

'The intelligence about where the conference will be held has also come true.'

Their LBs were supposed to be collected first, but after When's intervention, only their batteries were removed. Apparently their hosts do have a certain amount of mistrust when it comes to their peace-loving guests from the picturesque south. And when the elderly gentleman pulls a spare battery out of his pocket, it turns out that they are not so wrong.

As soon as a perfect hologram of Cologne Cathedral flashes up and illuminates the room with all its beauty, the diplomat realises for a moment that this might be a bit too big for him.

'The oldest building site in the world,' he mumbles, remembering his history lessons.

'Yes,' says Joseph. 'And the only building that didn't take a single bullet during the upheaval. None of the warring factions came close to the cathedral. When a bomb from the former armed forces almost hit the nave, some of the warring parties even joined forces for a short time.'

He wants to adjust his glasses until he realises that they have disappeared somewhere in the sunset.

I don't buy your senility, old man, thinks the diplomat.

'The place is sacred to all gaffs. The territory around it is conflict-free. No quarrelling. Not even weapons.'

Patricia and Katja smile at each other. The diplomat is also relieved.

So they can't shoot us down if we turn up there unannounced, he thinks.

'Reconnaissance has done its job. Now it's our turn.'

Latour looks round.

Jude prepares some pills. The boy seems to have checked what was on the table in front of him and is in the process of putting everything away. The girls are smiling wolfishly again, as if there will be free beer at the next carnival party. When has his eyes closed, Sras looks at the diplomat in silence.

Putting his hands together and shouting some kind of battle cry is probably out of the question today, Latour thinks.

The spy speaks up again. 'Everyone knows what they have to do. See you at the conference.'

Wordlessly, the medic hands him a few tablets, which he swallows. Then he faints.

Part Two
Who wants to find themselves

'I knew they were trouble. I felt it in my urine.'

Confused, the muscleman looks first at one of his mates, then at the other.

'Me too, boss,' says a guy who obviously had watched too many He-Man movies in his teens. The other just shrugs helplessly and grips his assault rifle tighter, even if there's nothing to shoot at.

Receiving no support from his followers, the man of the hour, because he is in charge here, he thinks bitterly, looks round the small square again. Perhaps he has overlooked something, he muses hopefully, after all it is still early and he has never been an early riser. But no, unfortunately it's the same as it was 15 seconds ago.

They are at the meeting point - the assembly point for the eco-tourists from Ontario or Alanya, he never listens too closely at briefings. The escort is there as well, their three vehicles plus the eco-scrap from the southerners, which has been patched up again.

But there's nothing to be seen of the Awarians, apart from a slight blond boy.

Joseph

The evening before.

All in dress uniforms, outside the hotel. Only the old man

seems to have suffered a collapse and is on his way to the hospital, which is not surprising given the stress of the last days.

His friends have wished him a speedy recovery and are pleased that the hospital has such a good reputation.

And that it is located in the city centre.

'You'll be fine,' said the nice doctor, smiling at him encouragingly. The nurses were also so kind to him, and the drivers were almost as funny as those at the ARK.

'Thank you very much, Doctor,' the old man had replied weakly. 'I hope I'll be well again in the morning. We have to make our way home. I think we'll be picked up at eight. I'm not from here, you know, and the stay is only until tomorrow.'

'I've already been told that,' says the doctor helpfully. 'I've already organised everything. Bureaucracy or not, you are a medical emergency and therefore fall within my area of responsibility. We'll have to observe you for at least another day. Don't worry, you don't have to go anywhere until tomorrow evening.' The doctor touches his arm in a friendly manner.

'That's very kind of you, Doctor. Thank you very much,' the patient replies hopefully.

Sras

'That's a wonderful story,' says the Cambodian woman with a laugh as she heads for the nearest pub arm in arm with the magistrate. 'I didn't think civil servants had such a sense of humour.'

Both have left the banquet early, before the Muuze. Apparently our contact was right, and this person does have more power than he was given credit for, Sras thinks, still looking amused.

'Well, I haven't been a civil servant for long. I come from the guild of craftsmen. So I don't really like talking that much. We prefer to use our hands,' he says, smiling ambiguously, which craftsmen don't really seem to be good at.

'That sounds excellent,' she says, dodging an attempted kiss so slowly that it almost looks real, while at the same time suppressing the reflex within her to return the proof of love with a gentle uppercut.

'Is that how it works here in Cologne? So fast?' she grumbles, even raising her voice accusingly.

'It's carnival, my dear,' he says with a laugh. 'Of course it's like this.'

She smiles shyly, which is about the hardest thing she has had to master this evening, but apparently it works. 'Surely you have private chambers where a lady is allowed to indulge in lust and still maintain her dignity?' Now she looks conspiratorial.

'I have a flat. Even with a view of Cologne Cathedral!'

She smiles gratefully and blows a gentle kiss on his artisan cheek. ' Really? That's wonderful!'

'Control centre, this is escort one. We have a problem.'

The boss waits for confirmation. His people have searched the hotel and found no sign of them.

The receptionist and the few maids - actually on their payroll and their eyes and ears - were no help either. Apparently no one from the banquet yesterday had returned to their rooms. Except for the boy, who stands smiling in the square with a bag over his shoulder, lonely and forlorn.

'Our visitors are gone.'

'What do you mean, gone?' a callous voice echoes from the radio.

Does this snooty secretary from the police station, who turned him down at the last carnival have to be on duty today? At least he is one of the few people who can even show off an original BMW with petrol.

'Not at the place we chose. They should leave today.'

'We know,' replies the bored voice and he imagines her almost simultaneously painting her nails and laughing at her LB.

'Are you talking about everyone?'

'No, there's one left,' he replies.

'Well, that's something. Question him. And everyone present.'

'We've already done that.'

'Then do it again.' The voice again, but this time faster, more uncompromising. 'We'll notify all units and hospitals. If our esteemed guests have been the victims of a crime, it will put our city in a bad light.'

And you too. Unspoken threats are the worst.

'Understood. We'll search the immediate area. We check the cameras and all means of transport. We'll find them. They are just a few grain eaters.'

'They've slipped through your fingers,' she reminds him coolly. 'And if nothing has been done to them, their disappearance can only mean one thing.'

Yes, he thinks, suddenly wide awake. Espionage.

When and the parcel

Yesterday again.

The joy seemed genuine, the diplomat remembers as he walks alongside When down a narrow alley. He himself is completely lost, but his brother seems to know where their destination is.

115

The magistrate - surrounded by a few other representatives of various guilds who had remained after the gun smoke had cleared - had thanked them profusely, repeatedly pointing at the three jute sacks that had been placed in the centre of the rectangular table formation.

And there really are three, the diplomat thinks, and remembers Sras's appreciative look when she realised that When actually had the presence of mind to get the bag out of the trunk before her kamikaze ride.

Well, at least now I know how to impress you, he thinks and a queasy feeling creeps over him.

'We would like to thank our guests from Awaria for their support. The fact that they have come all this way proves their loyalty and willingness to cooperate with us. The fact that they are willing to share their technology has shown us that even in these times, trust and friendship still count. Even on the big stage.' The magistrate smiled and raised his glass. 'We, too, hope to achieve the same level of peace, prosperity and progress in the not too distant future as has happened in the land of our friends.'

The brothers and sisters now also were beaming at their counterparts and raised their glasses. He saw genuine affection everywhere, really genuine, the diplomat realised, and he seriously wondered whether he might have only dreamed about the secrecy an hour ago.

He looked around and decided that he has done the people of Cologne wrong. The hall is nothing special and probably doesn't even have a history, unlike most of the buildings in this ancient city, but it is intact. And clean. Candles - probably in short supply here - have been set up. Even servants are there, bringing various dishes, even if the portions are rather tiny. Even the officials seem to be a little higher up the ladder, at least the third or fourth Princes´ Guard.

While the main actors got dressed up for the grand finale, Latour thought to himself and toasted to the magistrate appreciatively.

Then everything happened quickly.
He had already lost sight of Sras before the pastries and the medic was called to an emergency that had occurred near the hall. They missed the Halven Hahn, which the skillful chefs were actually able to make from pea extract. We really are blazing a trail of vegetarianism across Germany, thought the diplomat with a smile.
All who remained were the two Weithosen, who had somehow managed to get their stereotypical drinks, for which the diplomat naturally had nothing but the greatest respect. They had spent the whole evening with their escort, so that neither friend nor foe would be able to stand tomorrow. He himself had had a nice chat with the remaining grandees.
Then When had arrived, and something strange had happened to the diplomat.
Latour could hardly remember, so pleased was he suddenly to see him, and so nice did he suddenly find this party and all these wonderful, wonderful people.
He would have liked to stay, but When had just smiled at all of them, excused them both, walked out through the main entrance and left behind only people who found the world around them just so peaceful. And so wonder-, wonder-, wonderful.

There seems to be no end to the dark alley. Disguised and hooded figures walk past them. Some sway to match their pirate outfits, others still walk as proudly as their knight's armour demands of them, or still as weightily as their police officer slash security company slash inspector or soldier uniform demands - which is probably because they are real soldiers or police officers. Or were.

Latour swallows briefly and hopes that nobody notices them. A group of witches emerge from a packed bar, with brooms and ugly noses, the full programme. Among them is the one or other pretty one who can't hide her beauty.

If you only knew, he thinks as he is offered a shot of some brown liquid by one of the pretty uglies.

'Sorry about that. Not on duty,' he says with a smile.

When also declines with thanks as he has begun to fixate on a dark corner.

'And what are you dressed up as, you two cuties?' says another, who looks nothing like a witch with her pigtails and the artificial burns on her face, holding a candle, a red one.

'We're spies on a secret mission, but please don´t tell,' says the diplomat before he understands the costume. He looks at When with wide eyes and is glad that his brother can breathe better than him at the moment.

It has started to rain, but the fine drizzle is not enough to disperse the party-happy crowds.

When and Latour fight their way through the witches and their male companions, who are dressed up in rather new-fashioned costumes and shouting carnival songs even louder than everyone else. Now they merge with the corner of the house, which is not illuminated by the neon signs thanks to the low-hanging balconies.

It smells of urine, but luckily there's no one around at the moment who has chosen this place as a free toilet.

'Are you going to tell me what we're doing here?' asks Latour. Why has he gone through all the operational plans when there is something completely different on the programme every day anyway?

'Waiting,' says When unusually rude. By Awarian standards.

You're nervous, brother, he suddenly realises, and this thought makes the diplomat nervous.

'Do you think someone followed us?' the diplomat asks helpfully.

'No. Or rather, unlikely.'

'Good,' says Latour, looking helplessly at his non-existent LB.

Then, after a while that passes almost unnaturally uneventful, spotlights briefly sweep over them and the wall of the house, and Latour hears doors slamming as he closes his eyes.

Then suddenly a figure stands in front of them, about his height, slim, in a nun's robe, his or her face unrecognisable.

'You've made it. Good,' says a voice under the mask. Female, rather young, and almost a whisper.

Nice, Latour thinks, remembering the gentle hands of so many women and the soft voices that had woken him up in the morning.

'Follow me. Everything is ready.'

When nods almost mechanically before he can no longer feel anything. Except a fear like he hasn't felt for a long time. And bright, blazing anger.

'What was that earlier?'

The woman is gone without another word, as is the car.

Now they are in a room so close to the cathedral that they could stretch a yoghurt telephone across it. Spartanical, two beds, one window. A meditation cushion. A bathtub that is filled.

With salt water, as the diplomat notes, his skull buzzing like a swarm of bees.

'Nothing,' says When absently, while Latour searches the fridge for an ice pack. Or something stronger.

'I've just failed. Incredibly failed.'

When's version

I should have been prepared.

'What happened?'

A voice reaches him from far away as he gazes at the gloomy walls.

I am a guardian. We must always be prepared. For everything.

Outside, he sees towers that plunge into the night sky like pointed daggers. Dark gates that look more like gates of the underworld than gates of heaven.

'Are you all right, brother?'

The voice again. Eric´s affection briefly awakens him, and for a moment he wants to share the pain that overcomes him like the tide which is slowly drowning a flat rock.

'Yes. Thank you very much,' he replies, and manages a smile. But Eric recognises it, When senses as he looks into his new friend's eyes.

This man has no training, it runs through him again, but he quickly learns to read emotions, and more. To speak without words. And to look inside people.

So he retreats. 'I'm just exhausted.'

'As for that ...' says the diplomat, almost embarrassed. 'Earlier, when we left the party ... I know it was you.' He pauses for a moment. Takes a sip from a ludicrously small bottle of beer. 'Can any of you do that? Spread joy? So, purely mentally?'

When smiles gratefully, because he knows that all this is supposed to be a distraction. And indeed, it does work a little.

'Spreading peace it is. Peace is followed by contentment. And contentment is followed by joy.'

Latour offers him one of the ludicrously small bottles of beer. Ramsdorfer Kölsch. When hesitates briefly, then drinks.

'Yes and no. Everyone has the ability. The more often and more intensively it is trained, the stronger it becomes and the more people you can reach. I'll teach you.'

If I still can.

'You mean you have to.' The diplomat smiles. 'For our plan to succeed.'

When looks up, surprised.

'I couldn't help overhearing who the parcel is. And who should be smuggled in. With this trick. Don't worry, I won't take it personally.'

When nods gratefully. Then they both toast each other again and he goes into the bathroom. He takes off his clothes and slides into the cold, salty water.

Have I thought about you in the years that have passed? Yes. Too often, even by the standards of our friends, and far too often to be allowed to bear the name of a guardian.

But did I really ask myself the right questions or was I just dreaming?

Yes, he decides. He always dreamt of their reunion, but how bright everything was in his imagination, and how her eyes shone, and how tender her voice was; everything as if time had stood still. As if she hadn't disappeared, just with a last message - too long to leave him disappointed beyond recognition, too short to really matter.

'99.9 per cent of our existence consists of expectations,' he remembers his teacher saying.

Not Cremp, who only let his subtlety shine through once on

Christmas and Valentine's Day; no, Master Illuva, the one without a past.

'And most of these expectations are completely unrealistic when seen in daylight. In short: dreaming,' she had said, looking as compassionate as if she had known what her students would have to face.

And what can I do, Master, if this reverie, this woman, her embrace, her smile, her soft voice, even her coldness and anger are nothing but my own soul? If her existence is the blood that flows through my veins? That makes my heart beat?

What if all my efforts for our country, for our people and for peace are based solely on my love for her? What if I am afraid that without her there will only be coldness in me? And that anger will take over again?

'Brother? It's ... erm tomorrow. Shouldn't we ... do something?'

There's a knock on the door.

When opens his eyes. His skin has almost dissolved.

'I'm scared. I..am...so afraid,' he whispers - to himself or to his soul, he doesn't know.

Good, she replies. Then we can finally begin.

Preparations

He feels so cold that he no longer even recognises the difference between himself and the world.

Is there anything left of us when our senses stop working? When our skin no longer reminds us of the air, when sound no longer spreads its waves to remind us that there is noise?

And what if consciousness is too tired to remind me that I exist? Will I be sad, in the last moment, the last possible moment, or will I feel joy like never before?

'Good morning. Breakfast is on the table.' Eric smiles at him. Then he goes into the push-up, does a few repetitions.

'Thank you,' When says as he dries off and gets dressed.

'Oh, I didn't order this, but it's delicious. Apparently someone knows our taste.'

Or yours, corrects Latour himself, because of the lentil crap and all this food for future stuff. His breakfasts are often a little more sumptuous, even without women.

When smiles faintly, almost haggardly, Latour thinks. Then he walks past the table and looks out of the window, down at the deserted square and the cathedral, which seems as if it is holding its breath, knowing what is to come.

A rainy day, Latour knows, and wonders if it's good for them. For their operation.

But when he looks at his new brother, waiting in vain for the calm radiance to which he has almost become accustomed, he wonders if there will be any operation at all.

'You know our contact, don't you? That woman?'

Latour tries to remember how friends and relatives, sometimes his mother, sometimes his father, and sometimes the whole platoon altogether, started an intervention and tried to save him. From the arms of a femme fatale. He tries to remember a voice, admonishing, compassionate.

Until he realises that he never needed to be rescued. That he's never understood what binds people so tightly, whether it's to a place or a person.

So he tries to play the teacher without having the slightest idea about the subject.

'Do you want to talk about it?'

When turns away from the window. Adjusts his uniform. Breathes deeply.

And remembers.

'Nobody chooses these moments. Finding peace in good times is easy. Comfortable. Sometimes it almost comes to you. But finding calm in times of gloom creates true strength. Mastering these moments creates the guardians. It is not our birth that makes us special, not our possessions or our trophies, not our lineage or our looks. Only what we are able to do in those moments make us the chosen ones.

'Yes, friend. Thank you for your compassion. And forgive my weakness.' He slowly takes the meditation cushion and carefully places it on the bed. Then he places an ordinary cushion on the floor and takes a seat on it. 'I would be very happy to talk to you about it.'

He sighs and Latour suddenly has the urge to take this small, slender guy in his arms, so much he feels his burden weighing on him, or on himself, he doesn't know at this moment.

'But now is not the right time. It's a long story. It takes time, especially if an Awarian tells it.'

And there it is again: a smile, at least a small one.

'Besides, it's late and we have a job to do.' With that, he points to the cushion and gets into the lotus posture. 'Let's get started.'

Meditation

'Eric, please imagine a sound system. You sit-' When breaks off as he sees the diplomat swaying back and forth like a drunken sailor after a night of drinking in a filthy pub. 'Sitting cross-legged is perfectly adequate,' he says, smiling as he watches the diplomat try to get into the lotus position. 'It took me years to do it. As for the half-one. We are and will always be Europeans, even if the sitting postures come more from the East. It's important to have an upright spine,' he says. He thinks gratefully of his obnoxious teacher and places his two palms together.

Latour smiles with relief as he makes himself comfortable sitting cross-legged. Quite uncomfortable, he thinks, and is already longing for a really comfortable armchair - with or without a cigar and a whisky tumbler.

'This is going to be difficult,' he says, almost unconsciously, as his mind wanders off; first to the yoga teacher who taught his father - even including yoga instructions sometimes - and whom he secretly recorded in order to sell the videos to his mates for a lot of money. And yes, later on there were also one or two yoga teachers or yoga students, which taught him a thing or two between the sheets.

'... on your knees or on top of each other in your lap,' says When.

Latour frantically tries to disentangle himself from erotic thoughts, as pleasant as they may seem, and reconstruct what the boy, or should he call him master, has just said.

'By the way, I'm not a master. But since no one else is available, I'll take on this task.'

Jesus is no longer there. Buddha has also left, his masters had said, this time all of them, which was really a rarity, as divided as the rishis usually were.

But we are here.

We are here.

So we have to do the job, whether we like it or not. Waiting and keeping our mouths shut or keeping our hands off it because we don't think we're good enough, worthy enough, valuable enough is not an option. Cremp had drilled that into them time and time again. Who I'm going to beat up in front of the whole academy when this is over, thinks When. Even if I get kicked out of the Order.

'... okay.'

The master is now also trying to reconstruct what his pupil has just said, while defiantly pushing back the thought that not everything is going according to plan.

'But one more question. I mean, before we start properly.' The diplomat has no idea why he is asking so many questions. Maybe it's because his mind is already about to go supernova. 'Why now of all times? And right here? Wouldn't a beautiful Zen garden in beautiful Awaria be more appropriate? In a meditation group or ...' No Eric, you're not thinking of another pretty lady who you hope will show her thong during the lotus posture, for whatever reason ... '... with incense sticks and all that? And please, brother, don't tell me there's only one right moment to meditate.'

When smiles. Latour smiles back devotedly.

So that settles it.

'When we pass the guards, I'll make us both inconspicuous. We'll look so harmless that no one will really notice us.'

'Does that mean you'll make us invisible?' asks Latour, laughing.

'No. I can't do that. I'd rather say I'm making us so uninteresting that nobody will take any notice of us. You'd be surprised how selective our perception is. We don't notice some things that appear right in front of us. Other things, however, take up all our attention.'

'I see,' says Latour as he realises a few things. Things like his mind, and why his perception wobbles back and forth like a monkey that is always noticing something new and sparkling.

'I can make myself inconspicuous, and several brothers or sisters with me. At least that's worked a few times,' When says

with a smile and Latour knows that his young master is also re-
miniscing.

'And with a non-Awarian? Let's say with me, for example?
How often did that work?'

When takes a short pause that lasts far too long.

'If we both get into the cathedral unscathed? Then exactly once.'

Meditation (but now for real)

'Any more questions?' When asks helpfully, but Latour thinks
he hears a very, very quiet reproach.

Then the Awarian takes a few deep breaths that definitely
sound reproachful, the diplomat is sure this time.

'A few. But for the moment,' even he has noticed that words
like moment or now have a certain importance among the sisters and brothers, like gross domestic product, dividend and
growth rate in economy. '...I'm all ears. Or rather mind,' he
says, stifling a smile.

When laughs briefly. 'Don't worry, the path to tranquillity
doesn't have to be gloomy and sad.' He now sits with his eyes
closed, his voice getting softer and softer. 'Just a little silence
might be helpful.'

The diplomat refrains from responding. Instead, he does the
same as When and crosses his hands in his lap, his left hand
over his right. Then he takes a deep breath.

So far, so good, superboy. Then show me how to make myself
uninteresting. That would be something new.

'Imagine a sound system,' When begins again, his voice a mixture of soft singing and soothing background noise. And many, many pauses in the middle. 'Imagine you're sitting at the controls. You're listening to wonderful music. Some would say the sound of love, others the sound of silence. But ultimately it doesn't matter.'

The diplomat only nods now because he knows that the boy can sense it. Suddenly he feels the place where his heart is. Not all the time, but every now and then a wave comes, and a warmth flows through his body from there.

That is him. Like at the party.

'But what happens if we push the control all the way down?'

A pause. I don't have to answer, it suddenly flows through the diplomat's head like the little sailing boats he always liked so much on a Bächle in Freiburg on a summer's day.

I don't have to answer. I don't have to answer. I don't need to answer.

'The sound falls silent. And we hear nothing more of the wonderful music. You can compare this state to deep sleep. There's nothing there any more, noone to perceive and nothing that can be perceived.'

And some already consider this to be the final state, true enlightenment, When thinks briefly. And who can blame them?

But he let the thought go, even if he finds it difficult. But that would be too much for the first time. He realises again how important it is for a teacher to sometimes keep even important things away from a pupil.

'But it's far worse if we push the control all the way up.'

The diplomat understands. Or at least his head understands, because everything from the neck down seems to be slowly drifting along in a river.

We are suffering, his head thinks. Our ears are suffering. Our senses, our perception.

'We are suffering. Our ears are not made for this noise. We can no longer think, even our organs are rebelling against this over-kill. That's the state most people are in, especially in this century. The environment with all its radiation, its words, its messages and its machines makes it bad enough. But we make it even worse with our super-consciousness. Our addiction to absorbing and processing everything. With our desire for recognition. We never switch off.'

Silence. The diplomat no longer knows whether he can still hear When's voice acoustically, or whether it has begun to pulsate inside him.

I don't have to answer.

I don't have to think. I don't have to think.

'This control is our consciousness. And this regulator can be shifted. From absolute silence in deep sleep to absolute awareness. By us, do you understand, Eric? By us.'

The diplomat's head nods. It is getting lighter behind his eyelids. Perhaps the sun is coming out from behind the clouds. Which would mean that there is a real world behind his eyelids. But that doesn't have to be true, his heart thinks, because so much of what he has heard is not true.

I don't have to think.

I.

Must.

Don't.

'But we have forgotten. We'd rather travel to the stars than reach for the stars within us. We have to learn to control again. And bring it into perfect balance. To hear the silence again.'

Test drive

There is a knock.

Latour doesn't know whether to breathe a sigh of relief or to be annoyed. Relieved, as this day can hardly be surpassed in terms of passivity and boredom. Annoyed, as he seems to have just discovered silence for himself and has no intention of giving it up so easily.

He voluntarily gets up from the cushion he has been sitting on the whole time. Which was definitely too long, as he only feels a numb sensation where his bum should actually be.

There is another knock and a very polite voice apologises for the disturbance, but it will only take a few seconds, please open the door.

The diplomat looks at When. When smiles back at him, wide awake in a matter of seconds, something the diplomat will never learn, as he promises himself now.

'Your girlfriend?' Latour asks gesticulously, pointing first at When, then at the door, while imitating ridiculously exaggerated kissing manoeuvres.

When shakes his head and Latour almost thinks he has overstepped the mark for the little Romeo, but then he sees a faint smile. And is promptly served an answer when the Awarian points at the door, then at him, making completely exaggerated breathing movements and folding his hands.

Bastard, Latour thinks and smiles back, as confidently as he can.

There's another knock, now not quite so friendly anymore, and When disappears into the bathroom, but not without giving the diplomat a thumbs-up.

I don't know what that gesture stands for in your peasant state, he thinks, then stands up.

He breathes deeply.

And opens the door.

As if in slow motion, the door leans towards him.

Strange. No creaking, no noise. I didn't notice when I went in. And it opens inwards. Did I know that? I bet secret agents learn to look out for things like that. Sherlock Holmes certainly did. But he didn't even exist ...

First he catches sight of a beautiful foot in beautiful heels, which had already caught his eye when they received the keys. He had also noticed the woman before, receptionist and perhaps even head of the cleaning team.

Did the others notice anything? What am I actually wearing? Oh, the eyelashes aren't real, ma'am, but that's never bothered me before. Don't we all live behind a facade? And if so, what's wrong with a charming one?

He puts on his best smile, something he can do without being calm.

'Hello, how can I help you?'

The lady has also done her homework, he realises, because all impatience seems to have disappeared, leaving only the smooth cheeks and a charming smile.

A little too thick, my dear, he thinks, you haven't won any prizes just now.

'Mr. Hirschgang, I presume?'

Latour nods.

What are you talking about? You're the prize, buddy, the lady could have sent someone else. But she wants you.

'Yes,' Latour remembers, but so quickly that not even a detector could have noticed.

'I need your ID again. Just for a moment,' she says, almost apologetically.

'Is there a problem? I hope everything's all right,' he says with the kind of devotion and apprehension in his voice that he used to make teachers believe that he cared about their existence and that of the education system.

'No. Nothing special. The police have only issued a missing

persons report. Now all hotels are obliged to check on their guests. Your safety is of course the highest priority for our city and our hotel.'

'How kind of you,' says Latour, realising how much he has missed talking to people who have no supernatural senses.

'Do you know which poor soul is missing?' he asks, again concerned about these people who are now probably wandering the streets of Cologne all alone.

Slowly, he reaches into the bag containing the fake ID cards that When's little friend handed them before. Not perfect, not secret service quality, but not bad either.

'There are probably several missing persons. Unfortunately, I don't know anything specific. Just the names, which of course I'm not allowed to pass on.'

'Of course not,' the diplomat dutifully agrees.

Yes, make yourself an accomplice. Go over to their side. It's like the UN training programme for children. Oh man, kid, you can leave your magic tricks in the salt water. This will be a piece of cake.

His hand is reaching into his pocket, feels the emptiness inside and his smile disappears for a moment. Which is fine, the two gorillas who suddenly appear behind Snowwhite are smiling all the more.

They helpfully position themselves to the right and left of the receptionist.

No police. No weapons, Latour notices, but no regular hotel staff either. Probably a bit of hand-to-hand combat training, a weekend Krav Maga course, but certainly a gym session every other day.

Which could be an advantage if he has to run.

Yes, run.

Jump out of the window. It's just the ... I don't know, how many floors were there? Yeah, just one, just the first floor. And there's something under the window, I think.

'Are you all right?' Now it's the smart lady who looks worried.

'Of course. I just thought I had our ID cards in my pocket.' He demonstratively pulls his empty hand out again without having achieved anything.

Take her hostage. Break through. A life on the run sounds exciting. You and Snowwhite here. Or rather you and the Cambodian girl. Yes, I'd like that.

'Can we help searching?' asks one of the men, his voice surprisingly bright.

'No, no, my friend will probably have it.'

And what's his name?

He doesn't know whether he really has the famous beads of sweat on his forehead or whether he just feels sweaty.

Something with K. Something inconspicuous. Karl? What, the great one? I like Charlemagne better anyway, everything sounds better in French. When was the last time I actually ate an Andouiette? I-

Breathe, he interrupts himself.

I-

Breathe ...

'Kevin?'

No answer.

The delegation outside the door, fortunately still outside the door, begins to look almost embarrassed.

'Kevin?' he calls out again. 'Do you know where our passports are?'

No answer.

Son of a bitch! Answer me!

Answer me. OK then, don't answer. Everything will be exposed. What's going to happen? Nothing to me, my father will get me out. And nobody takes your peasant state seriously anyway.

So-

Breathe.

'Oh, my friend must have gone out while I was sleeping.'

Breathe.

'I understand,' says the receptionist less sympathetically as she reaches for her radio. The bodybuilders apparently smell action and pump themselves up a little wider.

Breathe. The silence. No worries, Eric. Just trust.

'I'm afraid I'll have to ask you to follow me then. The police will sort everything else out.'

I'm with you.

Then the door swings shut again.

With three more friends, as Latour knows.

It is only now that he realises the tension and consciously lets his shoulders sink and his head spin. Then he notices a figure behind him, cheerfully rubbing his body with a towel.

Latour takes a deep breath and regains a little of his calm.

Then he parks that calmness on his right fist.

And rams it into When's stomach.

'There you are, Kevin,' says the diplomat, striding past his slumped brother, pleased with himself and the world, and trea- ting himself to a flask.

When collects himself a little and gets back on his feet quicker than Latour would have given him credit for. He probably had to take a lot more from the kickboxing bees, Latour muses. That toughened him up.

'And the passports are where? If you were so kind?'

'How should I know that? You took them. I was in a ... dilemma, if you remember.'

The diplomat thinks for a moment. No, mate, you're not fooling me this time.

'I put them in my pocket. Where they should still be. So?'

'So? So I guess I'll have to go looking for them. I don't know why we're having this discussion. It worked, didn't it?'

'Yes. But they almost took us. You could have warned me.'

When puts the towel aside.

When did the room allocation actually take place for our trip into the blue? I've definitely been assigned to the wrong Awarian, Latour decides as he sees the boy naked for at least the 118th time that day.

'Ah, here they are!' the boy shouts triumphantly, fishing two small plastic cards from his uniform. 'I must have taken them at some point. Strange, I'm not normally this unconscious,' he says, smiling. 'Maybe I wanted to memorise our details. Above all, we should memorise the names.'

Memorising names shoots through the diplomat's head like a hot ball of fire.

'Breathe easily,' When says imploringly. 'And find the place that makes you calm.'

And suddenly it's there. The moment. And everything relaxes.

'Very good,' says When with satisfaction. 'You've found your place of stillness.'

'So to speak,' replies the diplomat. 'Silence is the only thing that counts, isn't it? What heals wins?'

When nods. He finds his friend's relaxed features almost a little eerie.

'Then I'm ... reassured. So to speak.' But I'd better keep the thought that's making me so calm to myself.

Sometimes everything is all right. Sometimes.

For Eric Latour, bon vivant, jetsetter, trendsetter, diplomatic starlet and ladykiller, the world is just one step better here and now on the bed in this small hotel room!

He looks contentedly at the screen, a real television with visible technology behind it, who would have thought? A Korean love series from the twenties is on, the English title sounding so stupid that the translator practically forces you to switch directly to the original Korean soundtrack.

On his belly, because he is lying on the bed, he has a large plastic plate with a real burger on it, with blood and tendons and real meat - salad and vegetables are barely visible under the quarter pounder, a view which he really likes. He takes a hearty bite from time to time and is fully aware of the fact that red barbecue sauce is running out of the corner of his mouth. And that his mate from Awaria is literally looking at him with a green face.

'Good thing I still had some foreign currency in my other bag,' says Latour, giving When a wry smile. The vegetarian is chewing on something that Latour´s burger once used to rub his bum on in a previous life.

'Is this some kind of punishment?' The Awarian seems genuinely confused. 'I told you, I can't remember exactly when and why I took the documents.'

The diplomat smiles patronisingly. 'It's not a punishment. Just pure pleasure! Besides, you don't need to apologise. I did a marvellous job.' He takes another bite, imitates one of the actresses as she politely curtsies and says 'Hello' in Korean, and gestures to When to bring him another one of those cute little beers.

Poor Koreans, he thinks, a shadow settling over his face for a moment.

She was fast, but not fast enough for all the countries in the world, and Seoul is unfortunately far too close to Pyongyang. Or was.

Later.
Neither of them looks at their watches, but they both know
that their stag party will soon be coming to an end.
 The November light is slowly fading, but the place around the
cathedral gets more crowded and some conspicuously expensi-
ve cars have already been pulling up.
 'It doesn't look like they're about to be baptised,' says the diplomat doubtfully.
 I'm sure I know some of them, he muses, but there's hardly any
chance of recognising details at a distance.
 'Shouldn't we, I don't know, take photos or something? Collect
information?'
 'That's not necessary. Kat and Pat have taken over that job.'
The diplomat briefly wants to ask where in heaven the two women are supposed to be, except perhaps in hospital with blood
poisoning. But then he looks at the Awarian, who is gazing
calmly out of the window, and he remains silent.

 Later again.
 Latour is about to say something, something that has been
bubbling up ever since he's been in such a good mood - because of the silence or because they are still relatively illegal, but
also rather undetected in a foreign city. What's more, they are
only a stone's throw away from a place where one of the most
interesting conferences Europe has seen since the Second
World War will be taking place in a few hours' time.
 'Listen-'
 But When interrupts him. 'There was a reason I didn't give
you a heads-up.' His voice is clear again, but quiet.

These people go from elated to heartbroken in a matter of minutes, the diplomat knows that by now.

'So you admit to the messup with the passports?'

'No. It was just a bonus. Whether I forgot or deliberately forgot, we'll probably never know.' He flashes a mischievous grin.

'So maybe there was a reason?' the diplomat asks, smiling venomously.

'Yes. We needed a first attempt. I needed to test whether I could connect with you. In an emergency.'

'You can't do that with everyone?'

'No. People can create barriers. Unintentionally or on purpose.'

'Well, I'll have something to learn when I get home,' says the diplomat cheerfully.

'We offer courses. Students not only have to learn how to open up to silence, but also how to block out the bad stuff. It's all part of our training. I will enroll you.'

'Very kind of you,' says the diplomat. 'So, did it work?'

'Very well,' says the Awarian, a little too surprised for Latour's taste. 'Minor difficulties at the start, but that's normal. Once you started breathing, it got better. You can imagine yourself as a boat on a stormy sea. I smoothed out the waves, you brought the boat into the harbour.'

'I felt more like I was just an antenna.'

'Also a nice comparison, but we like it more natural.'

'I see. So it's enough for the guards? To get us inside?'

When is silent for a moment. 'For the regular guards, yes. But there's a second hurdle we have to overcome. That's why I threw you in at the deep end...We have to get past the Guards of the Dome.'

'The Guards of the Dome?'

'Yes.'

'What are they? Something like car park employees? Do we have to pay admission to them?' The diplomat has to laugh.

When remains serious. 'No. They serve the Catholic Church. A ... special branch of the church, to be precise.'

Latour somehow doesn't like it when Awarians use words like special branch.

'Their mission is to keep people with bad intentions away from the sacred halls of the cathedral. The cathedral itself and the area around it are neutral, but the council has agreed on these protectors. And they have been fulfilling their task since the first days of the free city. And they do it very well.'

The diplomat looks through the window. It has become dark. 'And these cathedral guards aren't the kind of people we can fool so easily?' asks Latour, although he already knows the answer.

'No. They have a special kind of training. Combat training, of course. But there's more. Their students have been trained for decades by the elite of all Christian orders worldwide. Jesuit orders, but not only. They receive special training from an early age on. They have to remain silent for years, spend months in solitude. We are not sure, all this is secret. But we think that they ...'

'Using the strongest weapon available to us humans,' the diplomat finishes the sentence, folding his hands symbolically in prayer and suddenly realises why the Awarian is worried. 'You think they are like you.'

Battle uniforms

There is a knock and the diplomat tenses up again, expecting the next delegation, the next interrogation.

But when he looks into When's calm eyes, he opens and finds clothes on the floor, carefully folded and wrapped. He briefly looks to his right and left along the corridor, but no one is there.

'We must have had a delivery. Stylish,' he comments. How are you supposed to sneak in somewhere unmolested when you're wearing clothes like that?

Then he notices the pale envelope balanced on When's new uniform.

'And this letter, I think, is for you.'

Latour silently binds his bright blue tie. He can feel the price in the quality of the fabric and is puzzled. Apparently someone in Awaria has hidden a lot of foreign currency under their pillow.

He looks around the room, which now feels like his first own room, small but marvellous, mainly because he no longer had to share it with his sister. It had a skylight in the slope directly above his bed, from where he could watch the stars at night. This night here, tonight, is without stars, and even the moon seems to have disappeared.

'Are you all right, brother?'

He looks at When, who nods silently as he puts on the gala uniform. This time he's serious, Latour thinks as he sees the stars on his collar, of which he has no idea what they mean. Her picture is emblazoned on When's upper arm. In her last minutes.

And the first minutes of the new world.

'So that's it.' The diplomat scrutinises himself in the bathroom mirror and speaks as quietly as if he were talking to his reflection. 'I can't remember the last time I looked this good.'

'Yes.' When appears behind him.

'The participants must have gathered by now. We've got about thirty minutes left.'

And then another five until we know if it was worth the effort, the diplomat thinks as he fraternally adjusts When's uniform. Or we'll be mercilessly booed off the stage as the most embarrassing carnival troupe that ever existed.

'Enough time to read a letter,' he says, glaring at the boy.

The Awarian looks at the envelope, almost surprised that he is holding it in his hand.

'A letter in the twenty-first century? I think the effort should be rewarded. Don't you?'

When turns round and leaves the bathroom. Latour looks in the mirror again, smiles at himself, but doesn't quite manage it. With a sigh, he follows When into the room, checks the minibar and grabs the last two perfectly formed Kölsch.

'We really need to get out of here. I'm slowly getting used to the brew,' he says encouragingly.

But nothing happens, no movement.

'You can feel each other, can't you? You knew she was behind the door?'

When nods wordlessly. The diplomat looks down, then through the window. The cathedral is now in the spotlight, and if Latour ever felt that a building had a soul, it is now.

'Listen, brother.'

If I don't do something, we'll go home before we reach the

gate. I have to act. Get angry.

'I hear you.' Which is a lie, but at the end of the day, who cares about a lie?

'It brings everyone down. And you Awarians are only human. Strange people, but people.' He steps closer to When and looks him in the eye. 'If you ask me, your superiors choice of gathering intelligence lady was anything but fortunate. But if I understand you and your credo correctly, there's no need to think about luck. It's a hindrance. The causes lie in the past. They are over. So we should concentrate on the future, okay?'

And now the diplomat remembers his brother who, deep in the past, smoothed his hair and dried his tears when he was in love. Really in love.

'In the next hour, it is up to us to prevent the potential death and poisoning of hundreds of thousands of people. People like you and me. Children.'

When looks up and their eyes meet. For the first time, Latour has the feeling that he is not being illuminated by these unfathomable eyes, but that he himself is shining.

'But to do that, we have to do our best, give our best performance and let out everything we've been saving for a moment like this. Do you understand?'

The boy nods, and the diplomat feels a wave of friendship flow through him.

There you go, he thinks. I should have been a football coach.

'It's time to leave everything behind that could slow us down. We still have a good twenty-four minutes left. Enough time to get at least three love stories off our chest. You start.'

Burn me

When hands him the letter.
 The diplomat can remember all the gestures he's seen. Lots of signatures that have sealed the fate of countless people. For the better, and very often for the worse. To some of them, the smaller, more inconspicuous ones, he had even been present, and will again if tonight is their one-in-a-million lucky day. But his friend, Brother, who hands him the letter, leaves him speechless, even if he doesn't know the reason.
 'The title,' he says, looking thoughtfully at the envelope. 'It's not serious, is it?'
 'We Awarians try to put the past to rest or forget it - like you said. She's very good at it. She always has been.'
 'But...?'
 'But sometimes we don't succeed. Not completely. And then we write a letter that we don't really want to exist at all.'
 'I understand.' The diplomat nods. Then he opens the envelope, unfolds the beautiful white sheet of paper, revealing words in real ink that look like calligraphy.
 Latour takes a deep breath.
 'Any last words?' He grins at the Awarian, who just shakes his head.
 Last words alluding to.... the diplomat wants to say, but knows it's pointless. Apparently I've picked up my father's habit of covering up my own discomfort with a joke. I shouldn't do that.

 'When.'
 Latour frowns. No dear, no form of address? Just a name? Maybe that wasn't such a good idea after all. But one thing is clear ... I'm hoping for a few good lines and I'll stop the whole

story as soon as the emotional rollercoaster goes downhill.

After clearing his throat, he continues reading. 'I love you.'

He exhales. Well, that's a good start. These people just don't like to beat about the bush.

He watches his friend out of the corner of his eye. When looks relaxed, his eyes are closed. Latour wonders where the boy's mind is right now, as these three words are the magic formula for just about everything we have ever stored in our subconscious, both good and bad.

'I don't think it's necessary to apologise for the secret that has been made about my mission, because you will understand more than anyone else how necessary an insider is in a foreign environment, especially when so much is at stake.

To suggest that you have suffered during and because of my absence, or because of my professional demeanour and lack of displays of affection when we met again, would not only be self-serving, as if I would derive some pleasure from it, but also plain arrogant. You are who you are. How I got to know you. Your abilities, though not yet fully developed, are almost limitless, your tranquillity has the depth of the seas. And I am nothing but a wave that has glided fleetingly over your shallows.'

Latour pauses for a moment. Well, you've got it all wrong, sweetheart, he thinks as he tries to resist thinking about the ambiguity of her figurative language.

'So there's no logical reason to write these lines at all. Hence the title.'

I wish I had done it. Burned it. Or replaced the letter. I could have plucked something romantic out of my fingers. Or downloaded it from some poetry app. This one here is as loving as a tax document.

'But in the last few months, I've learnt that my training has proved inadequate. Not in terms of my mission. Apart from this letter, which is admittedly stupid, I have had some successes.

144

The mission would not have been possible without me.'

To anyone else, that would sound arrogant, he thinks. But she's right. And not just because of her taste in suits.

'No, my training has proved inadequate when it comes to you.'

Ah, maybe she'll get her act together after all, he hopes. He secretly looks at his watch, marvelling at how quickly the damn time flies when you're dealing with love matters.

'I'll spare you the details. Suffice to say that a glance at a 20th century romantic penny dreadful that Cremp likes so much would be enough to describe my emotional world. I would like to say that this only happened in times of unconsciousness, in dreams or daydreams. But it's not like that. Even in meditation - the heart of our country and our sanctuary, the place we both love so much - I had to surrender. The thoughts and dreams of you, of us, overcame me. I would like to apologise for this weakness. It is unworthy of our homeland and of you, my beloved. Please forgive me.'

The diplomat takes a deep breath, folds the letter and tries to look as impassive as possible.

As if the letter had ended with these words.

Nine minutes

'Thank you very much.' When folds his hands together and bows. No desire to reach for the letter. To see it with his own eyes.

Maybe I've been watching too many romance films, Latour thinks, pocketing the letter and trying not to exhale with too much relief.

'Are you all right?'

A few seconds pass. Latour has always hated these questions.

'I thought ...' Latour struggles for words, which rarely happens to him, but maybe you just don't have the words when you really have something important to say. 'I liked the ending.'

'Yes. And yes, it's all right. It is now.'

Brave how the young Awarian lies, Latour thinks. But When smiles again, and the diplomat almost has to laugh out loud as he gets his suit smoothed out and his collar straightened, this time by his friend.

'How much longer do we have?'

Latour looks at his watch. 'Nine minutes. Your friend knows how to be brief.'

When nods. 'Then it's your turn now, Eric Latour. In nine minutes, I'm sure you can get at least six more love stories off your chest.' He smiles. Mischievously.

'If that's enough.'

'Actually, there are only two.' And Latour marvels at how sure he is of himself. How little all his other lovestories have meant to him. 'My first love was when I was 17. I'd been in love before, but this girl really threw me completely off track.'

He remembers.

People often say that your grades would get worse and you would neglect your work. That wasn't the case for him at all. He couldn't get bad grades because he simply didn't go to school. He went into hiding. Dreamed about her. If she hadn't lived in the neighbouring town, he would probably have moved away, so indifferent was he to his physical presence anywhere at that time. And if it hadn't been for her appearing in some of his classes, he would have fled school, so unimportant did the monkey business about grades and subjects seem to him.

'Without her, I probably wouldn't have even graduated. After all, I had a good reason for it. I wanted to see her in her dress at the prom.'

When smiles.

And Latour is surprised at how clearly he suddenly sees all of this in front of him, as if he only had to push open a door to return to that time.

But he no longer needs to, he knows that now.

'I will make her an honourable woman.'

Their things are packed, even if there's nothing they couldn't leave behind.

'Who?'

'Your sister.'

'I only have honourable sisters. So you must be mistaken.'

The diplomat looks up briefly, thinking the Awarian is trying to fool him. But he just looks interested. They have lowered the blinds. Perhaps because they will see more of the old walls in the next few minutes than they would like.

'So ... I mean, that's what you say when you want to marry someone. And before you say there's no such thing as marriage anymore, I mean I want to spend the rest of my life with her.'

'I see.'

No mocking smile. These Awarians would make good couples therapists, the diplomat thinks.

'And by sister, do you mean ... one? Or two? Maybe Pat and Kat?' When enquires helpfully.

Latour is about to answer - inwardly he is already regretting the whole thing terribly - when this time he sees a mischievous smile on the boy's face.

Five more minutes.

At least one of us was helpful, the diplomat thinks, and starts again: 'Sras. I want her.'

'I know.'

The room seems so quiet to him, but it's not just the room. The whole city seems soulless, not even the raindrops can be heard anymore.

'Do I want to know my chances?'

'Let me think for a minute.'

He's serious, Latour thinks as the minutes tick by.

He almost has the feeling that the boy has fallen asleep while thinking. Which he couldn't blame him for, as he himself elevated this kind of thinking to an art form at school.

'Well, in my humble opinion, you have an above-average appearance. Your voice and the content of your conversation are also very lively. Your aura is clearly strong, as I noticed when we first met. Your skills in meditation are ... expandable, but existing.' When smiles.

'Thank you very much.'

Oh friend, you really have nothing to worry about, thinks the defiant boy of the diplomat. The dry When and his accountant girlfriend really are a perfect match.

'Your athleticism at least has potential, which also allows certain conclusions to be drawn about your qualities during coitus. Even if I tend to avoid that kind of speculation.'

You should have done the same this time, Latour thinks and feels like When has dragged him under a microscope.

'So?' he asks, as the Awarian has stopped talking again.

'That's why I think your chances with the ladies are generally good to very good.'

'That's ... er, nice to hear,' says the diplomat uncertainly.

'But as far as your particular choice is concerned, we have to apply a different standard, if you ask me.'

Latour sighs. 'And what would that be?'

148

'I only know Sras superficially, I must admit. If you want in-formation about her relationship status or former relationships, you'll have to ask her. Only she will be able to tell you about her past.' When pauses. 'But I am familiar with the Order of the Hand. And what its members stand for: Faithfulness, loyal-ty, discipline and dedication. All that is even more important to them than to the rest of my community.'

His voice maintains the same pitch, the diplomat notes as he nods.

'No one in my order is more committed to these ideals, and Sras places them above all else. Even above her own life. I think she expects the same from her partner.'

Latour nods again as he thinks back: to the crazy mob and the crazy Cambodian woman who crashed into it. Who let herself be beaten up to appear weak.

And suddenly he realises one thing: he has no chance. The im-possibility that he, a playboy who can pick up anything that doesn't get away fast enough at a cocktail party, won't stand a chance.

'I understand. Thank you, brother,' he interrupts the boy. Then he picks up his bag, looks at his watch and doesn't notice the sad look on the Awarian's face.

'It's about time. Let's go.'

The square.

The closing of the door, the few steps down the stairs and the encouraging smile of the receptionist pass him by. He almost wants to confess everything to her, so badly does he want an audience.

For what?, he asks himself as his gaze wanders through the darkness.

An ambulance is parked there, the lights are off. An old man

149

drags himself towards the cathedral, so slowly and pitifully that Latour would like to buy him a walking frame here and now.

Two women seem to be taking advantage of the night to have fun with each other in one of the dark corners. A lonely boy seems lost, probably a tourist, as perplexed as he is staring at a city map. A woman stands there, almost just a shadow. But Latour can sense her beauty, while at the same time wondering what she is doing here in her black dress and high-heeled shoes.

And the cathedral towers above it all. Even blacker than the night. The spotlights seem to glide off it. Lights shining from the windows seem to crawl, as if they are struggling to escape. And the figures, the gargoyles, the ones who are alive and the ones made of stone all seem to be waiting for them.

Panic spreads through him. He is cold, he is already soaked. And no one is there. No one.

Breathe.

No, we don't have ....

Breathe.

No, not this time. It's not working.

Where are the others?

He looks helplessly at his friend.

When looks at him with a smile. 'We should have thought of an umbrella.'

Yes, an umbrella. An umbrella. How simple and useful.

'That would have been nice.' Latour breathes a sigh of relief. 'But it's not that far.'

They set off.

So slowly that he can feel every bump in the square and distinguish the drops, feel their heaviness. Their lightness. Even a breeze.

'Wait.'

The Awarian stops, turns around to face his friend. His aura is already so strong now that Latour doesn't know if they want to enter the dome unnoticed or blow it away like the umbrella of a dandelion.

'Just one more thing. You asked me about your chances. I couldn't answer that, and I can't answer it now. But maybe it was just the wrong question. Maybe you should have just asked me about yourself. Then I would have answered that I have got to know you in this short time as someone who has depth. Someone who cares about what happens to this world and its people. Who stands up for his friends and often puts his own wishes behind. For the good of others.'

Silence. They both look down. See how rivulets join together in the stone cracks.

'If you're asking me if you have a chance ... I don't know. But I think you should try.'

The diplomat nods and looks at the Awarian seriously. The last few seconds pass. 'I will do that. And you'll get your girlfriend back.'

When wants to say something, but Latour looks so solemnly that the Awarian pauses. And silently nods.

'But first, let's get that fucking bomb.'

Part 3
Must first get lost

How many days have actually passed, the diplomat ponders as he feels warmth rising inside him.

And suddenly he sees the elderly gentleman at their side. This time with glasses again and with an energy which would light up a whole city.

'You've found a replacement, brother,' says When, walking on, feeling the spy's presence and bowing as he keeps his eyes closed.

Joseph nods at them, smiling. And Latour realises that he has missed the old fairy-tale uncle.

'Yes. The people here at the hospital were very kind and courteous. I'll come back later and apologise for the way I sneaked out in the dark.'

Ah, Latour remembers. There was something... sinister about this elderly gentleman.

'We'll put some of our best doctors at their disposal,' When says quietly, his voice getting louder and louder in Latour's head.

He looks to the front. A figure opens the doors of the ambulance, jumps out, and joins them.

'Jude. How nice. We were just talking about you.'

The medic nods affectionately at them. 'Brothers.' She is wearing the City of Cologne's paramedic suit, which looks beautiful on her.

'What do you think about instructing our new friends in one technique or another?' asks Joseph, almost in a conversational tone, and Latour asks himself whether they shouldn't start focussing, well, on that big thing up ahead that's getting closer and closer.

'That would be an honour,' says the young woman as she checks her numerous bags for bandages, syringes and things that will hopefully not be used tonight.

'Wonderful,' says the young tourist next to him. Apparently he has remembered his whereabout, because the map has disappeared and only a mischievous grin remains on his face.

'Brother Kwint.' Everyone smiles at him as the distance to the cathedral continues to melt away.

'Sisters. Brothers. What a joy to see you well.'

'How have you been?'

'Very well. At first, our escort was saddened by your disappearance, but that didn't affect my visa. From next month on, I'll be teaching electrical engineering here at school. How nice that their government has agreed to this.'

Everyone smiles at each other. Like on a bright picnic day, Latour thinks, as he can now make out the dark main gate more and more precisely; and the guards loitering in front of it.

The next two shadows that join their illustrious little circle don't even surprise the diplomat. Not even when Pat punches him in the side and he realises that he needs to sink a little lower to be mentally bulletproof.

'They can party here, there's no question about it,' says the little prizefighter in a raspy voice that Latour has almost missed.

How strange, he thinks. How quickly you can miss someone. I don't know if I'm in the right place, but what is a right place?

And the reason? With all the things that seem to be worth fighting for? That we are being forced to do? At least they haven't killed anyone yet, he thinks. Or at least he thinks so, as he lets his gaze wander over Kat and Pat once more. And then he sees her and knows one thing for sure: He is here with the right people.

Do people change when time passes?

Of course, Latour answers his own question. But do they also change when you think about them in their absence? Talk about them?

If so, I have been tranforming this woman into an angel for the last two days.

She smiles silently at the group, her stance resembling a motionless statue from a classical museum.

Unfortunately not so undressed ... Concentrate, you lecher!

She has swapped her high heels for light trainers within a second, which shouldn't really go with her dress. But of course it does.

'You're a little late,' she says and the diplomat feels as if he's hearing a female voice speaking for the first time.

It can't possibly be that they use the same sound waves as we do...

Concentrate, Petrarca!

'I thought I have to solve this little matter on my own.' She smiles again, wolfishly this time, and nods towards the entrance.

'It'll certainly be nicer together, sister,' Jude says, while the boy and Joseph just smile affectionately, When being no longer with them.

'You don't think you're going to beat up all those boys in there on your own,' says Katyusha, also affectionately, but with a certain ambition in her voice, as if she's about to carve a notch for everyone she wants to flatten in there.

'Well, you've already got a head start. Didn't you guys just bust up a Russian disco yesterday after smashing up an Irish pub? Sounds a bit over the top to me.'

'It certainly does. I didn't like the order either. But our escort was relatively ... persistent,' says Katyusha with a smile. 'And how was it with you, sister? Did you have a nice date?'

'Very nice. Unfortunately, my host was too sleepy and went to bed early.'

Then she looks at the diplomat. He wants to block out the date thing and her departure that evening - like a little schoolboy would do when he realises for the first time that he is not the only male on the planet.

Breathe. Breathe.

We have a mission.

Open yourself. Feel its power. Feel his power.

Feel your own power.

Slowly, the guards seem to be taking notice of them, Latour realises, as if through a veil of mist.

It's now or never, he thinks. And feels a hand grasping his. It is When. His thoughts are now as slow as locomotives that pull into a sleepy railway station twice a day.

Waves roll over him, over his heart, through his heart, and the small still pond inside him becomes a lake.

Then he feels his right hand being held. It is as if a silk serpent is wrapping itself lovingly around its victim. The pressure is so light, but he feels a force unlike that of When. Darker, eternally lurking. And ready to strike.

He opens his eyes briefly and looks into her eyes.

'I've missed you, Sras.'

'I know.'

She smiles, and he realises that the light in her eyes has always been there.

'Shall we then? I don't want Brother When to get impatient.'

The entrance

The moon.
 First it begins to stop returning the light given to it by its big, pushy sister. Then it slowly starts to break apart, to become a vortex of moon rock, from which piece by piece escapes the cycle and flies out into the dark space of the universe.
 The rain slides off his aura, which has covered him like a second skin. Not a physical skin, his teachers have always told him, even if you could use it in the physical world, which Cremp has always remarked on when he has harboured a grudge against the Sisters of the Hand.
 No, this aura is more like kind words begging the rain to lose its chill and spare this weak body, just this time.
 He fights the dizziness that briefly grips him whenever he stands upright instead of lying gently in a tank. But those days are over, dear When, he thinks, frantically trying to remember his name.
 'You'll have a hard time finding peace at the first stage,' the grumpy saint had always said, smiling almost pityingly. 'And then you'll find it. Why? Because everyone finds it eventually. Even you.' Then he was silent, secretly amused by his own joke. 'But after you've popped the corks and run up and down Lindwurmstrasse naked with joy, you'll soon realise that the second stage is even more difficult to master. Because that's where you have to fight not to get lost.' "And by fight," he said, 'I mean fight.'

How beautiful it is here.

This silence. Look, back there, a railway station. An old train with your name on it. And everyone who knows it, who could call you, insult you, love you, they all get on it.

And nothing remains.

He sways for a moment, only his reflexes keep him upright. And something else.

'Don't worry about your body,' he hears Cremp's voice again. 'Just as we don't stop breathing when we're not thinking about breathing, your body will continue to do what it's doing. As un-important as it may be.'

Another reprimanding look, even if he can't remember why. But some people have developed reprimanding into an art form - or a form of teaching.

'And as long as you are in this order, there will be people around you who will stand by you.'

Yes, that's something. There they are: a dark shadow with dia-monds for claws. A gentle melody, a wind blowing over moun-tain peaks. I am not alone.

I am ...

'So be careful. Don't lose yourselves completely. We have sis-ters and brothers who are specialised in bringing you back. But that can take time. And it's not always successful.'

I am ... Eric Latour? I am Sras Chann?

Am I a human being? Or energy? Yes, energy. It's so beautiful. So beautiful. These wonderful energies around me. Yes, even out there in front, far away, but not so much, these rectangular energies, locked and like short little waves, are beautiful in their own way.

Somewhere out there they are looking at weapons. Which aren't raised yet, but who knows.

Someone says something and muscles tense, on both sides.

You must not go yet, brother.

157

A voice.

You are When, and the humans need you.

Need you ...

And suddenly he feels himself again. And the energies swirl around him like a river swirling past sharp rocks.

Yes.

He opens his eyes. Smiles at the men who were four before, now nine, but what does it matter?

'We'd like to go all the way to the top if it were possible. Where the footballers are. From 1966,' he says, each word a small flash of lightning that invisibly illuminates the night; and muscles relax again, on both sides, because not even his sisters and brothers are a match for this strength.

Jude weeps, the old man ponders, and the rest lie in each other's arms - guards included.

Burning candles bring When back.

The rain has gone too. Perhaps forever, he thinks.

'Don't be surprised when, after you've travelled into the silence, thoughts that don't make sense pop up.'

If Cremp lingers in my head much more, I'll be charging rent, the Awarian tells himself.

'Distant pasts are common. Places you don't know as well. Or places you think you know. But you already know all that from Astro TV.'

At last the class laughs along, the few who have survived the last few weeks. Which is mainly because everyone in this town knows that the cranky saint loves Astro TV.

'But you can also experience ridiculously cheerful moments or be deeply saddened. Anything is possible. Whether the reason is that the brain enjoys freedom or is simply unable to distinguish between useful and useless thoughts, we don't know. Just get ready for an exciting time.'

Their footsteps echo through the corridors, which he had imagined to be larger. The air in here seems so old, as if it had been preserved and could tell stories from all the centuries past.

'You didn't tell me you'd been training in the meantime.'

A voice that is not his. A hand that lets go of him. Jude, tending to the mental aches and pains of the guards, who must have a lot to work through now that they've finally found their inner feminine side.

'And you didn't tell me you'd become so sentimental,' When replies again on the surface, which is also quite ok, and smiles at his sister.

Her make-up is gone, but only a little. And she seems to have shaken off the effects, he guesses from her soft smile. Unlike his friend Eric, whose head is so red that When asks anxiously if everything is okay with him.

'Of course,' says the diplomat, swallowing hard. He looks with almost inhuman composure past the woman he has just kissed under extenuating circumstances.

'Bring the level down. I understand,' Eric says almost accusingly, before a smile steals itself across his face.

'That was my plan. But it turns out that we really just look too good to go unnoticed. So I ...'

'Turned up the volume. To 'We'll annoy the neighbours ... From the next continent'.'

'I'd put it more modestly ...' says When, looking into Eric's eyes. 'But that sums it up pretty well.'

A hand rests on When's shoulder. Kwint and the old man have disappeared, probably having already bugged and video-monitored the entire cathedral in the past few seconds.

He sees Kat and Pat, who have started doing stretching exercises, which is show, When knows. Pleased, he realises that his sanity is somewhat intact again.

'How nice of you to use the time to get to know each other better. That must have been a great time in your hotel room.' Sras sounds amused as she steps between him and Eric, giving When a slight tug to look ahead. 'But I must interrupt you at this point. We have company.'

Her voice is low again as she looks towards the next patrol that comes strolling in their direction. Tailor-made suits. No visible weapons. Probably private security guards, one or two perhaps even with a degree in conflict management.

'I hope you haven't used up all your tricks yet, friend,' says the diplomat as he adjusts his tie.

'Let's find out,' the Awarian replies, dropping back down low into the sky.

Easy paths

The door is so beautiful, it looks more like a gate, thinks the diplomat. Have I ever been so happy to see a simple door? It's a bit strange that there are no guards at the entrance to Olympus.

A beautiful oak door, perhaps, and the most important thing: it's only ten metres away. More or less.

The last one of the Special Forces team from a secret mercenary training camp somewhere gives him a friendly pat on the shoulder and turns away.

'Honestly, When,' Latour shakes a few more hands, 'if I'd known how easy this was going to be, I'd have made myself comfortable in front of the TV and watched it all on the news.'

No answer. Just a slight tug in his head.

'When?'

No answer.

Latour turns round. Sees serious faces. The pulling gets stronger, you could almost call it a headache, he thinks, if we had time for this now.

Then he sees shadows, two shadows looming behind a pillar and approaching fast.

No guards, it flashes through his mind. I should have known.

'Sras.'

When looks at his sister, the walls within him shake. He breathes heavily, searching for his centre.

'I know,' is all she replies. She dives past him, and suddenly the diplomat is between the three women, field of vision obscured, which is perhaps better, because the headache seems to come from one direction.

'What is it, sister?'

The first time that Latour hears some uncertainty in Pat's voice.

'No time.' For a millisecond, she looks him in the eye. 'You only have one job from now on: if you see a gap, you run. Do you understand?'

'A gap. Why ...?'

'You run. You have to get behind that door,' she cuts the diplomat off. 'No matter what happens.'

Latour's head is ringing bells by now, but he nods.

Pat is leaking blood from her nose.

Then they turn round.

'The Awarians. We've heard of you.'

Two figures. In monk's robes, their faces hidden deep under

161

their hoods. They must have come from one of the side corridors, Latour tries to deduce, even if he sees no more side corridors in this area.

The air in front of them begins to shimmer and every inch he tries to push forwards is a struggle.

'Do you know that Awarie means catastrophe in Polish? Fitting, don't you think?' The voice drips with mockery. Yet there is nothing to stop it. 'Your mind has strayed from the right path. You are a mutation. As is your community.'

'This is holy ground. But you carry the demon within you,' the other figure continues. Female, soft voice, almost cheerful.

'Well ...' Eric struggles. The hope has gone out of him, he no longer even has the strength to stand upright. 'There aren't exactly the most peaceful lambs gathered behind that door.' But who needs hope when you can land a good joke?

Then the hood of the figure on the left falls. A girl no older than Kwint emerges. Delicate face, violet eyes.

'Wow. Now the church is sending little girls to fight their battles.'

'Eric,' When interrupts him. 'Don't.' His voice sounds like glass, with a small crack beginning to appear at the edge.

'Listen, kiddo. I know it doesn't look like it right now, but we're the good guys. And we want to do something very, very good.' His voice sounds like he's showing his little sister how to tie her shoes.

The girl stands there untouched, with real interest on her face. The other figure seems to fixate on the rest of the group. When has his eyes half-closed, the Hand's sisters stand ready in battle stance, breathing silently.

'So, how about this? You take your hooded mate now and let us through, then nobody gets hurt. And I'll break the bread at communion next time, I promise.'

'How obliging of you.' The girl steps forward and fixes her eyes on the diplomat. 'Eric, isn't that right?'

'I'm flattered,' he says sincerely. 'And your honourable name?'

'Do your friends know,' she whispers as she slowly approaches, 'that you are in fact Eric Latüne, son of Pascal Latüne, one of the worst people this world has ever seen?'

He smiles, but it gets harder and harder.

'That's what I thought.' She stops. Raises her hand.

'When, shield!'

Sras´ voice behind him. The Awarian doesn't move. The roar in his head gets louder.

'But worse than his evilness is your uselessness.'

'When. Shield!' Sras is shouting now.

When finally opens his eyes. Mumbles something, distorted, disfigured.

Latour struggles, gives the girl his best, hardest smile. Then she smiles back, and a red-hot iron runs through the diplomat´s mind as he falls, shitting and pissing himself, both at the same time.

Pathetic.

He is suddenly in his head. The voices outside become distorted, images blur in front of him. When's breath begins to crumble.

This power.

Fuelled by true faith, Awarian. Not from paganism and a few cheap magic tricks.

When's body staggers, his mind is surrounded by lava flows, parched by the shimmering heat all around like a dry twig.

Cremp, where are you? Illuvia? Why didn't you tell us? Where are you? Where is your advice?

They are not there, Awarian. Their existence, your existence, is like the ideas and techniques you learn so eagerly: they are all useless.

When wants to fight back, to bring his breath back under control. To dive back down into the still lake. But there is only a sea of burning oil that consumes all life.

And you are the glorious summit of uselessness, When. Just as useless as your sister has been.

'No!' When cries out. The walls inside him grow, a darkness spreads through him. Brief, but energised, it consumes some of the fire within him.

Forgive me, but I'm surprised how well your propaganda works. And how simple-minded you are.

Purple eyes glow in his mind, and the mockery in his opponent's voice burns like acid into When's heart.

You don't really believe in these stories? That a little girl was taken by the hand by angels and flew up to pluck all the nuclear missiles from the sky like a bunch of flowers?

One poisonous wave after another crashes over When until he falls to his knees. Sweat pours down his face, the salt stings his eyes.

That she died, When, petty and pathetic, that I believe you. And that your witchcraft has blinded an entire world. But we will end this. We will wipe you and your brood out, burn you out like plague. And we'll start with you.

Now there is only chaos in his mind. And grief.

Far away, he hears shouts, sees Pat and Kat running past him, towards their opponents.

He sees Sras bending over his friend, who is lying in his excrements, one hand twisted in wild convulsions. She strokes his cheek tenderly.

In front of him, far ahead, at an infinite distance - between them and the beautiful door - a fight breaks out.

I have to help.

I have to help.

I have failed. I can't make up for it. Everything is lost.

Tears begin to run down his cheeks.

I am powerless against such strength. I've let everyone down.

In front of him, Pat and the girl blur into a swirl of arms and legs. Next to him, Sras has carefully placed the diplomat's head on the stone. Then she looks at him. Just like his sister once did.

I have failed ... I cannot ... Everything is ...

'Don't worry, brother. Rest. Everything will be all right.' Then she looks ahead. And dust particles begin to light up and dance around her.

Close combat

'I'm going for Pippi Longstocking, Love,' says Pat firmly, giving Kat a serious nod. 'You'll get the other rag.' Then she steps towards the girl.

'Ah, the wild lovers. What a shame that something like you is allowed to run its disgusting mischief on this earth.'

Patricia focusses herself. Her world becomes a tunnel, at the end of which a sweet face awaits, not a light of deliverance. She is glad for this, because she wants to induce physical force in it until the speech apparatus is no longer able to utter a single word.

'And that mixture.' Every word from her opponent brings a wave, another gush of blood flowing from Pat's nose as the electrical signals take what feels like ages to reach her extremities.

Maybe I should have paid more attention to the voodoo training When and the others have been doing.

'Irish peasant folk meets Russian thoroughbred whore. How refreshing.'

Two more metres. The blood is flowing faster, the resistance is getting stronger. But so is Pat. Her muscles go into firing position, a bright sun begins to burn in her stocky body.

'The fact that a Russian hacker attack has shot your sorry high-tech economy back into the days of potato famine doesn't bother you?'

Pat pauses. Smiles.

The girl seems confused, for a millisecond.

'Bother me? Honestly? In every perfect relationship there are arguments. But don't worry, we always make up.'

Pat's first punch is aimed at the chest, but the girl is quick. She dodges to the left and responds with a precise punch to Pat's temple that staggers her.

Ah, welcome numbness, she thinks grimly. At least the headache has eased.

Two kicks hit her in the chest without her being able to dodge. But dodging isn't really her thing anyway, so she takes the hits. She responds with a straight kick that would have forced the beer belly through the throat of one of the stone saints, but the little girl dives sideways.

Someone hasn't just been leafing through old tomes, Pat thinks appreciatively as she backs away to avoid three lightning-fast kicks.

Did I just back away? she thinks angrily and catches her breath. Okay, princess, let's see if you're any good at wrestling.

'I'm really impressed,' says the girl with a smile.

The fact that her breathing is still steady and not a bead of sweat - not even blood - is running down her face, should cause the Irishwoman serious concern, if there was anything else she cares about at this moment.

'Apparently there's enough time between fornicating and sacrificing to paganism to do some exercise. You could get a lot stronger with us ... If you fill the pig trough every day and empty the latrines.'

Pat doesn't answer. She squats down, almost imperceptibly, concentrating on her centre of gravity.

'Like you said, Love, I'm a simple farmer's wife. Hard farm labour doesn't bother me.'

Then she shoots forward, faster than anything the girl has ever seen; she dodges once, twice, unleashes a hail of kicks and punches at her opponent, followed by a desperate headbutt.

But the Irishwoman breaks through, coming closer and closer until her arms circle the girl's body in a pincer movement; her hands find themselves behind the girl´s slender back. And lock her in.

Reinforcements

Katyusha walks slowly towards the rag, who is still standing there motionless.

Her body is a machine, only her mind moves. She dodges, blocks, turns to stone.

'Interesting,' says the figure. 'Not extraordinary, but interesting.'

'I can teach you. If you let us through. And call off your little friend.'

'I'm afraid that's not possible. But maybe I'll take you up on that offer. At some point.'

The rag makes a small gesture. Kat gets into attack position, hears stone grinding on stone, and sees more figures approaching from right and left. Dozens appear where there had been just a wall before.

She sighs imperceptibly, changing her foot position to 360 degree defence, if there is such a thing. Then she smiles in the direction of her friends, in the direction of the muscle monks.

'The church. I should have guessed. You just never run out of sheep.'

She wants to dash forwards and cut off the snake's head, use the rag as a door opener, but the team from the right is kind of quick. And coordinated. So she shoots towards the middle one and places a kick in the pit of his stomach, or hers, hard to tell. But no matter...she has no preference when it comes to who she sends to the mat. The upper body and legs come together helpfully, like a jackknife, before he or she goes down.

The flanks try to capitalise on the moment and attack almost simultaneously, one with a high punch, the other (her long hair showing under the cowl, therefore relatively certain to be a she) aiming a spinning kick at Kat's knee.

Still too early for the whole evening programme, she always thinks at such moments and leaves the combat splits in the holster. Instead, she jumps over the floor sweeper and kicks both feet so hard into the face of the punching man that she fears for a moment that his head will come off his neck and bounce through the cathedral corridors like a pinball.

Still in flight, she fires her fists at the floor sweeper, causing her to stagger without breaking her nose.

Okay, maybe I am biased after all, Kat thinks as her feet gently touch the ground again. Mea Kulpa, as her opponents would say so beautifully in Latin.

First row away; Pat rolls across the floor, as usual, and seems to be making real friends. Unfortunately, the rag is out of Kat´s reach. Does he get paid for standing somehow? she thinks, amused, until she sees the next row coming towards her. This time armed with sticks.

Nice. We're learning.

Down under

Somehow I think this is ... quite nice, Pat thinks as she slowly squeezes the breath and life out of the princess.

She really is very beautiful. Even if the shrieking is a bit unla-dylike. Why should I let go right now? And the headbutts? My dear, I don't have a mirror with me, but there's not enough of my face left to worry about after your spa treatment anyway.

She hears one or two bones cracking.

Those eyes ... Even more beautiful because weakness has fi-nally set in and they will close soon.

Wait, am I falling in love with this girl?

Then suddenly she sees boots, lots of boots, everywhere, hears battle sticks buzzing in the air, sees Kat out of the corner of her eye, whirling under the onslaught. When and the kind of hot fo-reigner are on the ground.

Oh, what the hell, she thinks briefly, and presses her bleeding lips to Pippi Longstocking's distorted mouth before the wea-pons come crashing down on her.

Observations from a ground perspective

Once nine is nine.

How strange, he thinks. He has never liked maths.

He opens his eyes and looks up - or at least he thinks that there is up there. But back when he was scubadiving and got vertigo, he didn't know which way was up and which way was down as well. There was just so much water wherever he looked.

Twice nine is eighteen, he ponders further, while his brain - now no longer in barbecue mode over a cosy campfire - does a little check-up.

He lies on his back, his pressure sensors letting him feel the cold ground too clearly, and something soft lies under his head. Or so he imagines.

Inside he feels somehow light, his body has taken care of that. His left hand is twisted, he doesn't know why, but the pain is okay, and he is right-handed, he thinks he can remember through a haze.

Three times nine is twenty-seven. And what's interesting about that, he asks himself? If only he had a piece of paper to write it down.

He realises that a tremor is still running through his body. But anyone who has had to live with restless legs syndrome for years has got used to the twitching and just hopes that a lady doesn't insist on an overnight stay.

And anything else? Yes, his face is wet, he must have cried somewhere on the way from the upright to the lying position. But that's okay, as this pain was rather ... unusual.

Now he remembers. This calm with When, then this terrible pain. This feeling of guilt, this shame that drove him to the extreme darkness of his existence.

Four times nine is thirty-six. Remember. The multiplier. One,

two, three, four.
When.
The ones.
Sras.
They always add up to a ten, a full ten.
Pat, Kat. The task.
Slowly his hearing returns. He hears voices. The veil before
his eyes disappears, the high ceiling looks down on him and he
sees bodies.
Attach a zero. Maths is easy, you fool.
And the door.
And pull the multiplier off again. Have you got it now, stupid?
'Yes, I have,' he whispers quietly.
Then you've slept enough. Look around!

His gaze wanders from left to right. Degree by degree, because
he doesn't want to attract attention. But it looks like he's not
playing a leading role in this lavish mummers' dance at this
point.
The last time I saw so many frocks was when I listened to Gre-
gorian chants in a church.
But the singers had no staffs with them. And they weren't beating his friends up either.
Through all the legs and bodies, he sees Pat lying on the
ground, a limp body buried beneath her, and a bunch of monks
beating her body unchristingly merciless. Kat tries to get
through to her, but wall after wall of enemies pile up in front.
Kwint and the old man lie where the walls and pillars used to
be, slumped and hopefully just unconscious.
Where is When?
Then he sees him, almost startled that he is so close behind
him, slumped over. Latour feels nothing more, no peace, no

calm, and knows instinctively that his friend has been taken out of the game.

Just like Jude, who is standing against the wall behind them with her hands up. Apparently the newfound friendship between them and the guards doesn't go quite so deep after all.

Killer like me

Well, that's going like clockwork.

He closes his eyes again. Breathes deeply, wishes he were on one of his father's many private islands - there'll be a lot of talking to do afterwards btw ... if there is an afterwards. Right now there is only a leaden emptiness inside him. No silence. Only sadness.

Do something.

I can't.

Do something. Think of the door!

It's so far away. So far.

A gap, she said. Look for a gap.

He opens his eyes. He turns his heavy head a few more degrees to the right and then he sees her. Walking through the attackers: calmly, slowly.

Two fighting sticks come flying towards her, swung by XXL size monks. One she blocks and breaks in the middle, the other she intercepts, balances its tip on her finger for a moment, then she thrusts it back, precisely into the attacker's right eye, like a master billiard player sinking a ball.

Two executioners, still beating Pat's body, and accidentally their sister's body underneath, as if they had to deal a certain number of blows as punishment, are caught by her from behind with two blows to the neck. Before they go down, as if in a duet, she pulls the two women aside and beds them side by side, while she absentmindedly flings the two freed torture rods over Kat's left and right shoulders and sends two more attackers to the bench (which sounds easier than it is, her sister doesn't exactly move slowly either,...but you know your kind of people...and their moves).

Then she straightens up. Some of the less tall acolytes back away, if only a little.

Ah, the war criminals are here, it suddenly echoes in her head.

'Does your order know about your past? Do they know you're a killer?'

The monk has pulled his hood off his head. Short, black hair emerges, pale skin, probably the little one's brother, the way his violet eyes glow.

'Do they know that your grandparents were Khmer Rouge? That you are a direct descendant of Tah Mok, one of the worst of them? And about the unspeakable crimes you all committed?'

Sras now walks towards him, floating through kicks, dodging blows. Her eyes are fixed only on her target.

The headache intensifies again the closer she gets to her opponent, but she knows this, her sparring against members of the defence force was too thorough and she should definitely apologise to them for her overly harsh reaction, she promises herself.

'Did they see the faces in Tuol Sleng? Your family always liked to brag about their torture methods.'

A few metres separate the two of them now. Sras breathes in.

173

The boy suddenly has two sticks in his hand out of nowhere; Nice trick.

'Harsh words from someone who is a member of an organisation that has tortured millions of people to death.'

She speaks, not wanting to enter his mind. She tenses up, fixes her gaze on a point behind her opponent's chest.

'But you're right about one thing: I am a killer.'

Crawling for beginners

Latour rolls onto his belly as inconspicuously as possible.

Out of the corner of his eye, he sees the security men approaching, guns pointed at the ground, which he thinks is a good sign.

They're enjoying the show, he thinks. I can understand that. Let's give the audience a proper finale, then.

By the way, maybe I should think more carefully about the decisions in my life, the really important ones, in the future.

He starts to crawl like he did in the army, machine gun firing height forty centimetres. He gets a metre away until he is grabbed by the feet. Suddenly he goes backwards. He is somewhat surprised when he looks round and sees a monk only half his size.

Latour tries to defend himself, kicking like a bug on his back. And it actually works. The fighting dwarf goes down. Okay, he thinks, the Taser that Jude hurled from ten metres - with her hands tied - and which then hit the hooded head with pinpoint accuracy, may also have been a reason for the decline of the Christian West, but his combat boots certainly played at least ten percent of the part.

OK, my first hit. He smiles at Jude, who smiles back briefly

before being knocked out with a punch.
 He rolls around again.
 So, where were we?
 Ah yes, crawling.

The next part of his Crawl to Canossa is no less than five metres, during which he wonders again and again how he made it
from his yachts and Ferraris to the floor of Cologne Cathedral.
 Deep down, am I an adrenaline junkie, he asks himself.
 Crawling works better now, at least he doesn't have to drag the
heaviest man in the platoon fifty metres from the field between
his legs.
 Then he suddenly screams as one of those sticks, which looked
so light and unimpressive, hit him in the back. He tries to ignore the pain - a phrase he will embroider on his shirt in future -
and crawls on.
 A second blow crashes down, followed by a scream and the
blows stopping abruptly. He hears a raspy female voice cho-
king and spitting in disgust, but continues to concentrate on the
path his warrior princess has cut for him.
 Or is this how I wanted to meet the one, very special woman?
If so, the plan had worked quite well.

Next stop: the place where the still upright wide trousers work.
What a stupid term from a stupid journalist who doesn't know
what a hakama is, Latour thinks. But why don´t these women
like fighting just against one opponent? Look at the Russian
woman. She is barely visible between the opponents who are
still standing.
 One of them becomes aware of Latour and tries to pounce on

him, but gets one of his comrades in the back and crashes into the nearest wall together with the aforementioned projectile.
 He briefly sees Kat's face in the mob and thinks he sees her smiling with her now colourful face.

Another eight metres. Maybe even less.
 He has made it past his future lover, and her opponent.
 The plan with the one extraordinary woman had definitely worked, he decided with satisfaction, even if he hadn't known about it himself at the beginning.
 For a moment he had considered playing the brave knight in shining armour, but then had come to the justified conclusion that, firstly, he wouldn't survive a second, as he would be felled in a flash by the stick man or her. And secondly, that he would be more like a rusty limpet on a scrawny nag, ruining everything that Sras has planned for the boy.
 He also had the feeling that even she had taken the time to give him a smile in the thunderstorm and form four words, at least the first of which had something to do with love. As for the smile, he had the same impression with Joseph and Kwint, who started rolling around wildly to distract his opponents, so it must be a mirage.

There it is at last, and finally within reach. The gate, only six metres away.
 Slowly, he crouches down. Trying to activate his muscles, what's left of them at least, and somehow, someway, prepares for getting past three more monks, armed with those nasty sticks and smiling, ready to fight.

The gap

He takes a breath. Straightens up completely.

They must be producing these monks on an assembly line somewhere in the catacombs.

He checks the flanks, but there's not enough room to run past, and he can't walk along the walls yet, but he's already written that on his list of future accomplishments.

And right through the middle? Difficult, apparently they've saved the biggest ones for last.

What the hell, he thinks defiantly. We've come this far, so I'm going to break through, no matter what.

He starts to run.

I will do it. For all those lazy bastards out there. For the children. And for this fucking peace on earth!

But by God, brother, I could really use your help right now.

You know what you didn't do right?

When's eyes are closed. Someone has put a pole around his neck and is holding him down. Another has thrown himself on his feet, which is unnecessary, as When is the only one who no longer offers any resistance.

No. I don't know. I don't know anything anymore. The teachings, the training, the silence. They are all gone.

Which is a lie, because the memories, all the painful ones, are still there; no, only they are there, drowning everything that once fuelled him, drove him.

You are arrogant, When. You always have been, even the moment you stepped into these halls.

'And my opponents have seen it,' he whispers.

Yes, When. Our opponents are always there to show us our weakness.

He squeezes his eyes even tighter. Tears that he didn't think would find salt anymore are pouring down.

'Arrogant.'

When, even the greatest sages had not the slightest chance of standing alone against their adversaries. We are only human. You are only human.

'She was only human.' Another whisper, but his opponents seem to have heard it, because they become more vigilant, their pressure stronger.

Yes, just a human being. A nothing. Small, powerless. Weak.

84,000 thousand reasons against us. When, everyone is bigger and stronger than us. And yet there is hope.

'Because we have an ally. A power.'

Yes, and you know this power. You have come to know it, in your darkest hours. Let go of your expectations. You will not achieve anything that is not meant to happen. Surrender to this power.

He breathes in again. But this time the air is almost like a melody, his whole body relaxes.

'I don't understand it. I can't do it. Never.'

And then he begins to smile as humility comes over him like a gentle summer rain.

The start of a sprint looks different, Latour knows that. And feels like someone who is standing upright for the first time after six weeks of bed rest. His tie has also slipped, which annoys him, as the three monks turn out to be three real nuns, with atypically muscular upper bodies, of course.

Three more metres.

His potential charge must look so pathetic that the three graces don't even get into fighting position.

Stop right there.

'What?' He slows down. A gentle warmth washes over his consciousness. 'When?'

Yes. Stand still.

He remains standing. If part one of the plan was to confuse his opponents, that part has already worked.

'And now?'

Nothing. You breathe. And walk. Slowly.

I'm with you.

Sras is so fast in his battle circle that the line between movement and teleportation becomes thin. But the violet one is also fast, very fast. Maybe because he's stopped talking. His sticks blur as they shoot towards the Awarian. She pulls up her forearms, tenses up, wants to break the toys with a block.

Then she senses that something is wrong. At the last moment, she brings her arms down, dives past him on the left and rolls off, almost clumsily by her standards. Out of the corner of her eye, she sees the two titanium bars clash like hammer and anvil.

Ah, this could take longer.

He falls.

The guards who have just beaten up the man who injured Jude begin to embrace her.

The expectations of his parents, whom he hardly knew, and those of his order fall away from him.

Those lying down - and there are many of them, as the cathedral corridor now looks like an emergency room - begin to help each other up. Awarian or cathedral guard no longer seems to matter.

The expectations of his friends fall away from him.

We are all just leaves in the wind, When.

Katyusha and the last two standing monks, tough guys, lie in each other's arms. Which they have done before, out of sheer exhaustion, but now it seems to be pure warmth.

Then he drops all of his expectations, expectations of himself.

The only thing we can do is dance with the wind.

When?

Sras takes a step back, then two. Her opponent now has the gaze of a hawk, focussed, ice-cold. Unlike her, because she feels a certain warmth and friendship, which she really doesn't need at the moment. When's waves don't seem to touch him. His fighting sticks shoot forwards in turn, as fast and in unison as the blades of a chainsaw.

Sras tries to find a gap, but there isn't one. So she backs away further, hoping that her opponent will fall over one of the bodies, which of course doesn't happen.

Suddenly a staff shoots forward and hits her on the shoulder. She screams and drops to her knees. Then he is already over her, her head the target.

She closes her eyes. When?

Yes.

Then the Awarian stretches out his hand, touches the monk's

foot and sends him back to a happy childhood.

Time to Shine

'Well then.'
 The diplomat straightens himself and his tie, remembers the
fighting parties he had been able to reconcile, remembers that
he had not done so badly.
 So off he goes, slowly but firmly, while trying to ignore the
raised weapons.
 'Trust,' he whispers, and breathes, bringing his breathing
rhythm up to the frequency of the waves flooding through him,
stronger than ever.
 Then he steps into their attack circle, tries to read their expres-
sions to see what will happen, but he only looks into petrified
faces that seem ... indecisive. Confused.
 He takes a step forwards. Says: 'May I pass, ladies?' and sees
them hesitate, then move aside, still with a confused look on
their faces.
 When, you old bastard, he thinks with a smile.
 And suddenly he's at the door.

You have to hurry, friend.
 'Yes.'
 Open. He puts his hand on the gigantic handle, looks back
briefly. His friends are all down, as are most of their enemies.
None of them would survive the next round, not even Sras.
 It will be locked. This is a conference. Of course-
 Trust, friend, When reminds him.

181

'Yes.'

Don't be locked. Please don't be locked.

The reinforcements have dropped to zero for the moment, but that won't stay that way, he knows. The guards are already approaching, wondering who they have to take into custody now and where the hell they're going to get all the stretchers from. And the three prayer sisters also seem to be wondering about what has just happened.

Open!

Latour takes another deep breath. He thinks of aeroplanes like shooting stars in the night sky. Then he presses the door handle with almost a tender push.

'Ladies and gentlemen,' he begins in a somewhat croaky voice, but who can blame him?

He doesn't remember how he made it to the centre of the hall, only that it took his whole body strength not to fall into the room with the door. Now he feels only exhaustion - and astonishment, because surprisingly few weapons have been drawn, and he is still standing here, surrounded by very powerful people. Usually, he would start with a joke and smile mischievously at some of the ladies, while winking secretly at those in power. But those days are over, he realises.

'You only have to remember one thing when you're standing up there,' his old teacher used to say to them when Latour couldn't sleep before a presentation or was worried sick about the lecture. 'People can give you a hard time beforehand and they can tear you apart afterwards. But when you're up there, when you have their attention, it's your show and yours alone. So make something of it.'

Well, he thinks, I've got their attention, that's for sure. And I'm still standing. So let's go.

'My name is Eric Latour. I'm part of the diplomatic mission of the Free State of Awaria.'

Silence. Some people wrinkle their noses and he knows why.

He breathes in slowly, feeling the tranquillity welling up inside him like a silent river, and knows that this time it's not When, no, it's his own personal silence.

He looks down at himself. Breathes out.

What the hell. Babies piss and shit all the time, and everyone likes them too.

'Our country is dedicated to peace. To the peace and happiness of every single person, every single country, every continent. Therefore, we humbly request permission to participate in this conference. Please give us the chance to preserve peace in this beautiful land.'

He then bows deeply and folds his hands into a wai.

The end

Apologies and words of thanks

Even though it is obvious to any reader that this book is the product of my imagination alone, I still feel obliged to make a few apologies in the spirit of Awaria and its quest for harmony. I would like to begin with an apology to the whole of Germany. Our homeland is beautiful, I knew that beforehand. But I only realized how beautiful and harmonious it is, even if it doesn't always look like that, when I had to use every ace in my sleeve to destabilize this country and create a kind of "Wild West" for my heroes (so it wouldn't get boring). But instead of finding a breeding ground that can't wait for violence and hatred to grow on it, I realized during my research that from the far north to our beautiful south, villages where people are there for each other are lined up with cities so big that peace amidst the skyscrapers seems almost an impossibility.

Yet all this exists, and I can assure people, especially those who do not yet know Germany and hopefully visit us one day, that the chances of encountering a medieval army with machine guns or a wild mob attending a witch-burning are relatively slim.

So visit our adorable Alter Peter and Cologne Cathedral and of course the Wilhelmsturm in wonderful Dillenburg; go shopping in Siegen before the military make the City- Gallery their headquarters. Hike in the Königsforst and travel through such wonderful communities like Abbenroth and Amtsknechtswahn (they really DO exist).

You will not regret it.

Finally, my deepest gratitude goes to a dear friend in beautiful Colombia. You supported me from the very beginning, Cathy. Maybe I could have done it without you...but it would have been very difficult. The Spanish translation will follow at some point, I promise.

I have saved my last thanks and apology for my editor Maria. My thanks because without her help the book would have languished on the brink of incomprehensibility, and my apologies because I was unavoidably defiant and selfish and insisted on my chaotic and incorrect syntax far too often (but I'm a writer, I'm allowed to do that).

If a halfway readable middle thing somehow emerged from this, it would be almost unbearable;)

© 2025 Thorsten Schelberg
Publisher: BoD · Books on Demand GmbH,
Überseering 33, 22297 Hamburg, bod@bod.de
Printer: Libri Plureos GmbH, Friedensallee
273, 22763 Hamburg
ISBN: 978-3-8192-7832-7